Pocahontas jumped to her feet. The emperor restrained her with a heavy hand, with what must have been an Indian oath. She flung his hand aside and embraced me. Presently men in yellow robes appeared from out of the bitter smoke and violently tore us apart.

In fear of our lives, Soltax and I hurried from the scene, past the sacrificial fire and the piled stones of the altar. At the temple door I stopped and looked back. Pocahontas was being led away. Would we ever, ever meet again?

Also by Scott O'Dell:

ISLAND OF THE BLUE DOLPHINS
THE BLACK PEARL
THE KING'S FIFTH
THE DARK CANOE
SING DOWN THE MOON
THE CRUISE OF THE ARCTIC STAR
CHILD OF FIRE
THE TWO HUNDRED NINETY
ZIA
CARLOTA
KATHLEEN, PLEASE COME HOME
THE CAPTIVE
SARAH BISHOP
THE FEATHERED SERPENT
THE SPANISH SMILE*
THE AMETHYST RING
THE CASTLE IN THE SEA*
ALEXANDRA*
THE ROAD TO DAMIETTA*
STREAM TO THE RIVER, RIVER TO THE SEA*
BLACK STAR, BRIGHT DAWN*

Published by Fawcett Books

THE SERPENT NEVER SLEEPS

A Novel of Jamestown and Pocahontas

Scott O'Dell

FAWCETT JUNIPER • NEW YORK

RLI: VL 7 & up
        IL 8 & up

A Fawcett Juniper Book
Published by Ballantine Books
Copyright © 1987 by Scott O'Dell

Library of Congress Catalog Card Number: 87-3026

ISBN 0-449-70328-2

First published by Houghton Mifflin Company. Reprinted by permission of Houghton Mifflin Company.

Manufactured in the United States of America

First Ballantine Books Edition: January 1989

20 19 18 17 16 15 14 13 12 11

to Bob and Tennie Bee

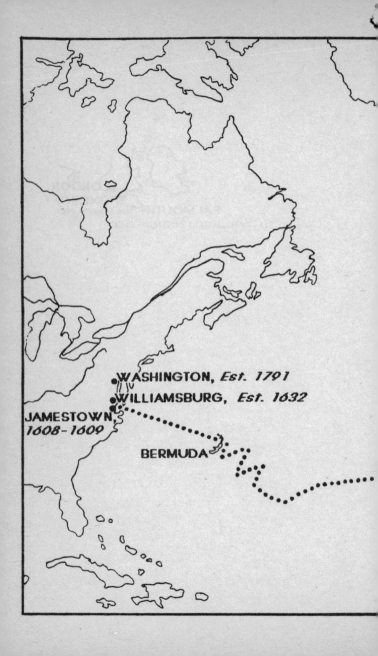

WASHINGTON, *Est. 1791*

WILLIAMSBURG, *Est. 1632*

JAMESTOWN,
1608-1609

BERMUDA

LONDON
FOXCROFT
FALMOUTH PLYMOUTH

CANARY
ISLANDS

Voyage of the
Sea Venture
and the
Deliverence

1609–1610

BOOK ONE

Foxcroft, England

One

Foxcroft lies among green meadows where sheep graze and wooded hills abound with deer. The River Dane flows lazily around the castle, holding it in a fond embrace. Walls of rosy stone spring blithely toward the heavens. Flags fly and golden weather vanes turn round and round.

It seems a peaceful place, where one happy day foretells another. And so it was until a stormy dawn when my brother and I were fishing on the River Dane. Not fishing, really, but poaching on the part of the river that belonged to the earl of Covington.

I didn't like to fish and I had never poached for fish. Poaching—catching fish in waters that belong to someone else—is a serious crime. You can have an ear lopped off, or even your head.

My brother, Edmund, was the keeper of Foxcroft's fine horses, thirty-three of them, which was a very responsible position. But he loved danger and he loved to fish. Poaching was a nice mixture of both. Besides, Lord Covington's two miles of the River Dane boasted the deepest pools and the best currents for leagues around.

The night before I went to the river with him, Edmund

came up from the stable just as I was going to bed. He stopped me on the stairs that led to the tower where I slept and did my work.

"I need your help," he said.

"With what?"

"With fishing. They're getting suspicious at Covington. I almost got caught last week. I had to throw my fish in the river and run for it."

"What can I do?"

"Tomorrow morning I fish Covington's. You're needed to keep lookout."

I began to tremble. "What happens if we get caught?"

"If you keep your eyes open, we won't."

"But if we are, what happens? You go to the jail, then I lose my good place at Foxcroft. And who knows what the earl of Covington will do? He could call out the bailiff and cart me off to jail."

"Nothing like that. He's not a vengeful man."

"Most surely he'd tell the countess."

Edmund untied his red neckerchief and gave me a contemptuous look. "One thing about you, Serena, I don't understand is why you're such an infernal mouse. You didn't get it from Mam or Dad. They're stout people. Probably from your granddad, the biddable preacher, who raised chickens to eat but was so chicken-hearted he made someone else kill them."

Edmund tied his neckerchief and stalked down the stairs. When I reached the tower, I watched as he went down the path to the stables. I was angry with him for saying what he had—for saying I was an infernal mouse. He had called me that name before. A dozen times before. I was tired of hearing it. I was undressing, but I put on the clothes I had taken off, ran down to the stables, and told him I would go with him in the morning and keep watch.

At dawn I met him on the river. It was a stormy day with

black clouds tumbling over hill and meadow. Covington Castle, atop a rocky crag, stood hidden, but the road that led to the river showed clear.

"They're sowing timothy below the castle," my brother said. "It's early yet but they'll soon be coming down. Keep watch and tell me when you first spy a cart."

He cast a hook into a pool of roily water, and I took up a place nearby where I could talk to him and watch the Covington Road at the same time.

He had been fishing for only a moment when his line tightened and ran off the reel.

"I've hooked a monster," he called out. "Two stone it will be, maybe more."

"More, the way it pulls," I called back. " 'Tis surely a prize."

The current ran dark after the night of heavy rain. The line came in slowly. It wrapped itself around a floating tree. Edmund, who was good at fishing, curved a loop, freed the line, and took in what he had lost.

The sun struggled up, casting a murky light. The Covington Road showed clear.

"There's a stump yonder," I said. "Not far in front of you. It's sunk deep and it's mean-looking. Four branches sticking straight up."

"I see it," Edmund said impatiently. "Watch for carts. I'll do the fishing." He went up the river a short ways and guided the line around a stump, took in the slack, and wound in slowly. The line sang, sending off drops of water. For a moment it went slack in a quiet way and floated. We both thought it had come apart.

"Lost it," my brother said.

"Too bad! But we can try again tomorrow," I said to raise his spirits.

"The big ones are old. They're old because they've learned and gotten smart. This one won't strike for a while. Never, most likely."

Suddenly the line tightened and the big wooden reel rumbled. Half the line went out, down the swirling river. The pole bent double. Edmund hung on and a foot at a time got most of the line back. Off it went again in the roily current. Again he got it back.

There were sounds from the west. I told him that I saw a cart leaving the Covington Gate. "We are within plain sight," I told him.

He got out his knife.

As he did this, a great black cloud hid the sun. It was dark again on the river. Edmund put the knife away. I climbed a small hill nearby where I had a better view of the Covington Road. The cart had disappeared.

When I came back to the river, he was reeling in, guiding the fish through tall weeds close to the shore.

It was then that I heard voices in the woods behind us.

"It's not the Covingtons," Edmund said. "I know their voices well. But best we not chance it."

He took out his knife and cut the line, and the fish swam away. The voices grew louder. A pack of beagles, their tails held high, came charging toward me. I heard branches snap and the sound of hoofs. I saw a band of hunters break through the willows.

Ten of them, strung out one after the other, carrying guns. In front was a tall, pale-faced man in a peaked hat. From the clacker and small horn around his neck I took him to be a flusher.

"A very good morning to you," the flusher said.

At least that is what I thought he said. I am not certain about this, for he spoke with a burr. His words sounded like hard lumps of coal tumbling down a chute. He was an odd-looking man for a deer flusher. Huge around the middle but with long, spindly legs, he reminded me of the actor I had seen play Shakespeare's Falstaff.

I thanked him for his greeting and wished him well. My brother was walking on, bent dejectedly against the wind.

"Fishing poor?" the flusher asked.

"Beastly," I answered, to put him off.

"It's not the right time of year for salmon, though some run to the east of here."

He went on, naming the streams where fish might be caught, speaking quickly and with a burr. I only half-listened, anxious to be at work.

"You seem but little interested in the fishing sport," the flusher said.

"To me, 'tis not a sport. I'm sorry for the fish. I prefer to let them stay where they be."

"You have tender thoughts," he said. "Too tender for this world. How do you fare in life? How do you possibly manage? What do you do? Raise silkworms in a cloister? Do the munching worms distress you?"

"I work for the countess of Foxcroft," I said, wishing he would ride on and attend to his hunting.

He got down from the horse and came toward me, limping a little. He was not the huge man, the famed Falstaff I had envisioned. It was the ponderous quilting he wore from hip to stomach, a custom among those who lived in fear of a dagger's thrust, that made him appear the size of two.

A curious thought weighed upon me. I asked myself if I had seen this man before, the scattered beard turned gray, the spindly legs, the tongue too big for his mouth, the piercing eyes set far back. I had.

From a close distance I had seen him six years before, on the day he traveled through Selby Village as King James the Sixth of Scotland, on his way to London, to be crowned King James of England. I was a child then, yet I well remembered the jeweled gentleman on a jeweled horse, surrounded by a crowd of lords and ladies.

Two

Any doubts I might have had about the identity of the man limping toward me were soon dispelled. A tall, strikingly handsome youth came out of the woods, put his arms around the man, and kissed him on both cheeks.

"Your Majesty," the youth said, "we flushed eight deer, fat ones. Seven doe and a pretty buck. They're below us, sire, by the river."

"Thank you, Carr," the king said.

I knew that Robert Carr was a gentleman of the king's bedchamber and, among many young gentlemen, his favorite.

"Sire, the deer will scarcely wait," Robert Carr said.

"Of course they'll wait, aware that they have a fateful meeting with the king," James replied, and fixing me with a piercing eye, he said, "Where do you belong, young man?"

He wasn't to blame for calling me such. I wore high boots, with my skirt tucked up, and my long hair bound tight and hidden under a headpiece of rabbit fur earlaps.

"My name, sir, is Serena Lynn."

"Ho," he said, drawing close to have a better look. "And what do you accomplish at Foxcroft? Something

8

lithesome, I dare say, judging from your white hands, the noble breadth of brow, the hesitant tilt of your head, as if you were not quite sure what this life holds for you."

"I read to Countess Diana. Her sight is poor."

"Yes, quite poor, but the only thing poor about the lady."

"And I write letters for her."

"Social letters?"

"Mostly, sir."

"Did you write the invitation to a masque in honor of somebody or other, two months from now, the thirteenth?"

"Yes, Your Majesty."

Carr cleared his throat and said, "We cannot attend. We'll be hunting in the North Country on that day."

"Whereabouts," the king asked, "do we hunt?"

"At Arondon Lodge."

"Oh, yes. I had luck there last year, didn't I?"

"Six stags in less than a day, sire."

"And another wounded that ran off."

The king drew closer and said, "Perhaps, Miss Serena, you'll write me about the masque. Who was there. Who kissed whom. Who got drunk and fell in the river—and so forth. I like gossip. And I like your writing very much. Your words move like a file of my grenadiers, marching across the page under kingly banners."

I thought of telling him how I had come to have such stately handwriting, that I had been born lefthanded but my teachers had insisted that I use my right hand, which resulted in the letters slanting neither to the right nor to the left, but meeting as desired, smack in the middle.

"You write letters. Now tell me, young lady, what do you read to Countess Diana?"

"I read your beautiful book of poesy and another book of yours, the book named *Demonologies*."

At the word "demonologies," the king's face changed. The piercing eyes grew fearful and sought mine.

"I am told there are some hereabout. Demons, haunts, witches. Have you met any?"

"None, Your Majesty."

"That's good to hear."

He brightened and glanced up at Foxcroft Castle, where a shaft of sunlight struck the many windows, its chimneys and turrets, the clockhouse rising above the rooftops.

"The castle has a bonny look," he said, "peaceful to the eye."

" 'Twas peaceful once, not long ago," I was emboldened to say. "But not now, sire, not now."

"You speak distressfully, grow pale. What disturbs Foxcroft and you?"

"Countess Diana's son has gone."

"Who? Gone where?"

"Anthony Foxcroft has been taken away. He's in London in jail, in the Tower."

"On what charge?"

"For libeling the king."

"I know nothing about it. I do not feel libeled at all. Should I?"

From the moment I knew I was in the presence of the king, I had thought of little else. It was a wonderful chance to speak on Anthony's behalf. But now with the chance thrust upon me, with the king waiting to hear what I had to say, I could only stare at him and say nothing.

Robert Carr spoke up. "Anthony Foxcroft has been brought before the chief magistrate for saying he wished the Gunpowder Plot had succeeded. And you, Your Majesty, had been blown sky-high."

This was an outrageous lie. It shocked me to my senses. "Begging your pardon," I exclaimed, "Anthony Foxcroft never said this thing."

Carr lifted his gun and took aim at a passing bird. "How do you know?" he asked.

"I was present when the story was told. It was meant as a joke. There was much laughter. The mayor of Wentworth laughed and so did Carew, lord deputy of Ireland. Everyone laughed."

The king turned his eyes upon the castle. "What, what?" he said. "Anthony Foxcroft in London? In the Tower?"

"It all happened," I said, "at a masque given by Countess Diana to celebrate Guy Fawkes Day. Anthony told a long story about Fawkes and the Gunpowder Plot. How the conspirators had dug a tunnel under the Parliament building, and had filled it with iron bars, fagots, and thirty-six barrels of gunpowder. Set to go off the day Parliament was to open."

"I am acquainted with all this," the king broke in. "What did young Foxcroft say that brought him before the chief magistrate?"

"Yes, what?" Carr asked, annoyed at me. "Quit rambling!"

Now that I had found my tongue and the king was listening, I was determined not to be hurried.

"Anthony stood beside his mother, by the big fountain, in front of a hundred guests, and said—I remember his words, every one of them.

" 'Can you imagine this moment?' he said. 'After a long and dangerous effort a tunnel has been dug. It's filled with gunpowder. Enough to blow Parliament into the heavens and back, along with every minister, the lords and their retainers, even the king himself. The conspirators have planned an escape once the powder has been set off. Horses are ready along the line of flight. Houses are waiting where the men can hide as they flee. And what transpires?

" 'We have a curious scene. The door of the cellar that stores the gunpowder stands open, on the theory that an open door allays suspicion. And in front of the door walks Guy Fawkes, sword in hand, mustache abristle.

" 'The earl of Suffolk, who is in charge of the houses of Parliament, happens by, having heard rumors about a plot. At the bottom of a stairway he sees an open door and decides to enter. He finds a cellar stacked with fagots, enough to fuel the city. Out he comes and says to Fawkes, "What is it? What's the purpose of all the fagots?"

" ' "It's firewood," Fawkes mutters. "Belongs to the earl of Northumberland."

" ' "Huh." Suffolk grunts and leaves.

" 'But at midnight he returns with a group of deputies. In their stockinged feet they creep down the stairs and find Guy Fawkes in front of the open door. He struggles like a madman and holds them off, but they subdue him. Beneath the fagots they find powder, a long train of it winding through the mound of wood.' "

Robert Carr and the king were still listening.

"At this moment Patricia, the Covington daughter, said, 'What would you do if you wished to blow up Parliament, all its ministers, and the king?'

" 'I've never given it much thought,' Anthony replied.

" 'But if you did,' Patricia persisted, 'how would you go about it? Would you dig the tunnel secretly and tell no one?'

"Anthony closed his eyes and said, 'A jug of water stands beside the king. He always has a big thirst, which arises from the drinking of too much sweet wine. I'd dress myself in a servant's uniform, walk in, and pick up the jug. If anyone asked what I was about, I'd say I was freshening the water. Then I'd take the jug out, empty it, fill it with gunpowder, and take it back.'

" 'Oh, my!' Patricia said. 'Then you would light the fuse, run out, and change your clothes. Then everything would blow up—the building, the ministers and their retainers . . .

" 'Not everyone. Just me and the king.'

" 'Oh, not the king!'

" 'Yes, he'd be flying along right beside me.' "

I cast a quick look at His Majesty, not at all sure he would like the picture of himself flying through the air. To my immense relief, he was pounding his chest in glee.

"Clever," he gasped. "Clever fellow, this one. When I wish to have someone blown into the sky I'll send for Anthony Foxcroft."

The king drank deeply from a wine flask he took from his doublet and, after a moment, instructed Carr to see that Anthony Foxcroft was released.

"A mistake, Your Majesty," Carr objected. "Foxcroft must be taught a lesson. We'll introduce him to the rack."

The rack was an ancient device which the king had improved since the time when he ruled the Scots and wished to rid the land of witches. Those he condemned as witches were fastened to the contraption. Wheels were turned, and as they turned, legs and arms and joints were slowly stretched out of shape, inch by inch.

"Show it to him, at least," Carr said. "And introduce him to the leg iron."

This was a clamp, an invention of the king, which fit the leg from ankle to knee and was screwed tight gradually, snapping the bones.

"Foxcroft's an arrogant fellow," Carr said.

"Arrogant, like all the young," the king said.

"Arrogant now, a conspirator later," Carr said. "Nits grow up to be lice."

I tried to stifle the cry that rose in my throat. To no avail. As it echoed in the meadow, Carr gave me a curious look.

"Why does the fate of this arrogant youth concern you so much that you cry out like a wounded stag?"

I didn't try to answer.

"You gave us Foxcroft's story with great emotion. Tears were in your voice. You wrung your hands. A pretty act, my dear, a believable story as you imagined it, but one far from the truth. You should be an actress and play Shakespeare's sad Ophelia.''

Still I did not answer. The king noted my silence. "No more of this," he said.

Robert Carr took heed. Smiling, he said, "I ask your pardon, miss. I did not know until this very moment that you were in love with Anthony Foxcroft. Had I known, most surely I would not have expressed myself in this fulsome way. A thousand pardons!"

"Enough," the king said. "Send word to London by yonder squire that Foxcroft is to be released."

Robert Carr stiffened as the king fixed him with a look of one who was sent by God Himself to be His voice here on earth.

"Move upon this at once," the king said.

Carr hesitated. He had beautiful pink and white skin. Lustrous auburn locks framed a girlish face with a small red mouth that he set in an angry pout upon hearing the king's command.

A brief contest of glances followed. Then the king said, "Move or else you will be the worse for it."

Robert Carr bowed stiffly and went off at a leisurely pace to deliver the message which he did not like at all. When he returned, the king asked where the pretty buck and the seven fat doe were hiding. Before Carr could answer, a horn sounded and a herd of deer broke cover. The buck brushed past me, so close I could feel its hot breath.

King James aimed his gun and brought it down with a single shot.

"Bravo!" Carr shouted. "For three days you haven't used your gun, yet you shoot with your same deadly ease."

The king laughed. He was very proud of his skill as a huntsman, and I knew that he hunted whenever he had the chance. When he came to England to be crowned, surrounded by thousands of admirers, he spied deer grazing in a pasture, leaped from his horse, and killed three. And as soon as he was crowned, he started off with his gun to visit estate after estate to kill more.

Retainers shouted "halloo," took out their sharp knives, and busied themselves with the carcass. I started off to find my brother, who had edged away, but the king grasped my arm and led me to where the sharp knives were flashing.

He scooped up some of the stag's blood, washed his hands in it, and spread some on his padded chest. Reaching out, he daubed my forehead with a bloody finger.

Shocked, forgetful that I stood in the presence of a king, I recoiled at his touch.

"It is a talisman," Carr explained.

"More, much more," the king said.

He climbed up and stood in the steaming carcass. In the mist that swirled about him he was truly a kingly figure, as if he had taken some strength from the blood of the slain deer.

"'Double, double, toil and trouble; Fire burn, and cauldron bubble,'" he said, quoting from *Macbeth*. "'Twill burn the witch's brood," he added, quoting himself.

Scrambling out of the carcass, he wiped his hands upon Carr's silk doublet. From his little finger he took a ring and slipped it on the middle finger of my right hand. It fit perfectly.

Carr frowned, albeit he must have grown used to the king's generosity. It was well known throughout the land that His Majesty liked to dispense to his favorites pretty baubles and fine jewelry, also hills and rivers and castles. In one generous afternoon, he had created more than thirty knights, twelve barons, three dukes, two earls, and a handful of baronets.

"A princely gift," Carr explained. Then, taking my silence for ingratitude, he said, "Stand not like a little churl. Open your pretty mouth and thank His Majesty."

Summoning my breath and all my wits, I did so and made something of a curtsy besides.

"You will see," the king said, taking my hand, "that the ring you wear takes the form of a serpent. The serpent's coiled thrice round in a circle, thus depicting the soul from birth to ascension. You will also see that the jeweled eyes are half-closed. Do not be deceived. Neither night nor day, in all of life's strange maneuvers, do the eyes ever sleep. Beneath their hooded lids they silently observe, and upon what they observe, should it threaten your life, they quickly act."

The king dropped my hand. It burned. My throat burned. My forehead burned.

"Guard the ring well," he said, "and it shall guard you."

"From what?" I stammered.

"From harm."

"From all harm? Forever?"

"Forever, but not from all. There are many harms, too many. Not from those that arise from jealousy and from greed, especially. Only from those that threaten your precious life shall my serpent guard you."

"And guard you it shall," Robert Carr said, aware that I was puzzled. "The serpent ring is the king's magic mark and sign."

His Majesty placed a hand upon my shoulder. It was a powerful hand, a sovereign's hand. His dark eyes rested upon me. No longer soft and wandering, they were eyes of a king. He had changed. Had the blood of the slain stag changed him? Was it now coursing through his veins?

Silent under his spell, I stood transfixed. At last I opened my mouth. "Thank you, thank you, sire," I stuttered.

The king nodded and turned to Robert Carr. I made out little of what he said, for his words came rapidly, both in Latin and in French, mixed up with blood-tingling oaths.

He paused, wiped his beard, which he had drooled upon, and gave me a message for my mistress.

"We've changed our minds," he said with a sly smile for Robert Carr. "Let Arondon wait. Inform Countess Diana that we'll attend her masque."

Carr mumbled something under his breath, but the king went on.

"We'll be there if not pinked by an assassin's knife or befouled by a coven of witches. And tell the countess not to trouble herself about food and shelter. Pavilions shall be brought for all. Victuals and varlets to prepare them. Robert will see to everything, won't you, dear boy?"

I desperately wanted to ask him when Anthony Foxcroft would be freed, but I thought the better of it. He had promised to come to the masque. Certainly he wouldn't come if Anthony were still in custody. I bowed, albeit my knees tried to betray me, and was about to leave when the king grasped my hand and pointed to the ring.

"You tend to be a fearsome lass," he said. "But fear no longer."

Struck dumb, I bowed and, without so much as a word of thanks, fled from his presence.

Three

The shot the king had fired and his blue and green banners afloat in the meadow had brought the castle to life. Heads showed at every window as I ran up the path. Countess Diana herself was on the terrace, pacing back and forth, trailed by a crowd of servants.

I ran up the long flight of steps and arrived in her presence gasping for breath. "The king's in the meadow," I stammered. "I talked to him only two moments ago. Imagine talking to King James of England! He talked on and on, just like a person. He asked me questions. He admires my handwriting. He sent, he sent you . . ."

I had to pause for breath. The countess reached out and gave me a shake. She was short, immensely fat, and very, very strong. Her fingers bit hard.

"Sent me what?" she said calmly.

"A message. Anthony is free. And the king is coming to the masque!"

She jumped to her feet and threw her hands in the air and danced in a circle. Then she sat down and caught her breath and smiled, showing her dimples, two deep ones on each side of her mouth.

18

Countess Diana smiled a lot, whether the word was good or bad. The year before, for instance, when word had come that three of her ships had been lost in a storm off the African coast, with all the crews and more than two hundred black slaves, she smiled and said, "I still have three ships left."

She grasped me by the wrists. "Are you sure that Anthony is free?"

"The king sent a message to London to attend to the matter."

"What a boon! The news lifts my heart!"

She released the grip on my wrists. Her sharp eyes took notice of the smudge on my forehead. "Blood," she said. "A gift from the king?"

"Yes. Just now in the meadow after he killed a stag. It's a talisman, Robert Carr said. The king said it is much, much more. But I am puzzled. What can it be?"

"His Majesty believes that standing in the open body of the stag gives him strength, which he needs, having a crooked leg. He also believes that the blood with which he washed his hands and daubed your forehead has power. It is a mystical power that opens the door into a secret world. You believe in none of his nonsense, do you?"

I scarcely heard her question. My head was going round. I had seen the king of England. I had talked to him. I had stood close enough to touch him. I had seen him send a messenger to London to free Anthony Foxcroft. He had invited me to come to London. Upon my finger I wore his magic ring. His pledge rang in my ears.

The countess gave me a disgusted glance. "You must believe in the king's nonsense or you would not be in such a swoon."

Before I could answer, she caught the sultry glow of the circlet His Majesty had given me. She grasped my hand. She drew me aside because servants were listening, slipped the ring from my finger, and examined the inward side of the gold band.

"I make out a unicorn," she said, more to herself than to me. " 'Twas His Majesty's sign in the days he was king of the Scots. Where did you find it? In the meadow, by chance, where the king was hunting?"

"I didn't find it. It was a present from the king."

Squinting, she stared at me. Her pale, near-sighted eyes darkened. "Why would the king give you a ring? A ring of any value? For what possible reason? Now don't lie to me, don't you dare! Tell me the truth."

"We were talking and the king asked how I was employed at Foxcroft and I told him. Later he gave me the ring."

"His Majesty and I are friends," she said. "Clearly he gave you the ring but meant it for me, to make amends for holding my son in jeopardy. With such a valuable gift, he could not have dreamed for a moment of anything else."

She had rings on every finger, even her thumbs, and she tried the circlet here and there until she found a finger where it fit. She held her hand up to the struggling sun and smiled. Then she squinted at my forehead again.

"Go to your room," she said. "Take a big handful of soap and wash off the bloody stain. 'Tis of no use against witchery. Or for that matter, against any of life's mischances. Nothing is, save common sense."

"I shall be glad to wash it off, Countess. 'Tis very uncomfortable."

"Please do so at once!"

I went to my room and washed the mark away, using two handfuls of scented soap. Yet, strangely, when I combed my hair in front of the mirror as I got ready for breakfast, the mark had not disappeared. It was in the middle of my forehead, right where the king had traced it with his jeweled finger.

For fear the countess would send me back to my room when she discovered that I still carried the king's mark, I decided to eat breakfast in the kitchen, not with her in her bedroom as I usually did. Later, I'd work on the spot with the harsh yellow soap the servants used for the dishes. But I had no sooner reached the kitchen and begun to eat than she appeared, leaned over the table, and squinted at me.

"You've rubbed the skin off," she said. "The king's ugly mark is gone. An odd man, King James. When he comes to Foxcroft he always hunts by the river, as you know, and appears covered with blood. Do not quail if he wishes to daub you again. Appear honored, make a bow, and thank him. I hope you did so this morning."

"I don't know what I did."

"Did he give you the ring before or afterward?"

"Afterward."

"Then you didn't insult him. He insults easily and doesn't forget. Remember my advice when he comes to Foxcroft for the masque."

"I shall."

Countess Diana, who had decided to eat with me in the kitchen, picked at her smoked herring. She ate like a bird. I often marveled that she could look so much like a female Buddha on the morsels she carefully selected to put in her stomach. I marveled, too, at her son, who could consume platefuls of venison and suet dressing yet remain as thin as she was enormously fat.

The countess divided her smoked herring into three pieces and gave them to the three piebald cats weaving in and out between her feet. "You told me that the king laughed," she said, "when he heard the story, and that he told Carr to see that Anthony was freed. What did Robert Carr say?"

"Carr advised the king to keep Anthony in jail for a while. At least to show him the rack and the leg clamps. He said that Anthony was an arrogant young upstart and needed a lesson—that nits grew up to be lice.''

"You'll remember the two of them quarreled here at Foxcroft. That was two years ago at a masque. I've forgotten what started it, but Carr challenged Anthony to a duel with two-handed swords. Anthony, because he is not a swordsman, refused the challenge. Then he challenged Carr to a duel with pistols, which Carr refused. They don't like each other, which is unfortunate, because Robert Carr is the king's favorite.''

"I was terribly afraid all the time we were talking that the king would take Carr's advice and give Anthony a scare.''

"Anthony has needed a scare," the countess said. "He's become something of a monster, a sweet monster, 'tis true, but a monster nonetheless. He seeks out danger, hatches quarrels the way Sir Walter did. He's as arrogant as Raleigh was when that swashbuckler was young. He adores Raleigh. He even had a painting of Raleigh in his room, where he could see it when he awakened in the morning. And a pair of Raleigh's rusty swords, which he bought in London, crossed just so and hung up beneath the painting.''

She picked a crumb from her plate and studied it, trying to decide whether to put it in her mouth.

Hunting horns blew in the meadow, and I heard the sound of galloping hoofs moving away toward the south.

"I think the king plans to bring a large party to the masque," I said. "But he says for you not to trouble yourself. He'll bring tents, victuals, and cooks.''

"The king always says that. Last year he came to Covington with one hundred twenty-five and stayed for a week. Twelve of his guests, and most notably the earl of Southampton, his lady, and their three children, were afraid to sleep in a tent. Sir John Lambert of Edinburgh and his two daughters had bad colds and couldn't sleep in tents. A baronet and his guest were sleeping in the carriage house.

Isn't 'baronet' a silly title? The king invented it, and now we have as many baronets as there are fish in the sea."

The sound of hoofs faded away. Countess Diana ate the crumb she had been toying with, licked her plump fingers, admired her new ring, and after a while said to me, "Considering why I present the masque, searching your deepest thoughts, what do you suggest for the subject? Something historical, don't you think? But nothing Greek or Roman, and I have done one about Malik al-Kamil, sultan of Egypt, and the English crusaders."

She got up to let the cats into the wine cellar, which lately had become the home of a horde of long-tailed, green-eyed vermin. As I went on with my breakfast, I gave serious thought to the question.

Truthfully, she was presenting the masque for one reason: to raise funds for the Jamestown colony in Virginia, which was in the gravest danger. Settlers were dying like summer flies—three and four a day from ague, starvation, and Indian arrows. Pitifully, fewer than a fifth of the one hundred ten who went out in 1607, just two years before, were still alive. Another winter and nobody would be left. Like Sir Walter Raleigh's settlement in Roanoke, the colony would be nothing save ashes and sad memories.

But the countess's concern about Jamestown and its dying settlers did not arise from a soft heart. It came from a very hard head. She owned shares in the London company that furnished the ships, collected the settlers, and sent them off on a four-thousand-mile journey across the sea. Shareholders hoped to gain profits from the plentiful resources in the New World. They knew of the vast tracts of fertile land, forests, winding rivers, clear lakes, rolling hills. They also expected to receive gold, and lots of it, and shiploads of silver, too.

Friends and enemies alike mistook Diana. The sly smile, the pretty dimples, the childish voice, all were apt to deceive. But beneath the mounds of pink flesh her spine was made of Damascus steel, and in her veins, it often seemed to me, flowed the blood of a dragon.

She was born a commoner and a beauty. Before fat engulfed her, when she was only plump, she caught the eye of the earl of Foxcroft, a very wealthy man who had made a fortune gathering slaves along the African coast and selling them to the Spanish planters in the West Indies.

When the earl broke his neck chasing a little red fox, he left his fortune and a fleet of three seaworthy ships to Countess Diana. Instead of selling the fleet and living a life of leisure at Foxcroft, she surprised many by continuing her husband's practice of gathering slaves along the African coast. In a short time she had doubled the number of ships and the business among the Spanish sugar cane growers in the West Indies.

The problem now was money. Seven ships lay anchored in Plymouth Bay, one of them furnished by the countess. Five were provisioned and ready to sail, but two were empty. At least seven provisioned ships were needed to rescue Jamestown's starving settlers. Countess Diana's purpose in giving the masque was to sell her guests shares in the Company of Adventurers and Planters of the City of London for the First Colony of Virginia, as it was called.

Now she was at the cellar door, having trouble with the cats. They were full of smoked herring and did not wish to stalk green-eyed rats as big as they were. Instead of calling a servant, she called me, and the two of us got one of the cats into the cellar whilst the others escaped.

We went into the Great Hall, sat by the fire, and talked until noon about the theme for the masque. Some twenty years ago, Sir Francis Drake had sailed from Plymouth. He raided the Spanish coast and returned with goodly treasures, a Spanish galleon in tow. There was no better theme for raising money than to celebrate Sir Francis and his daring feat.

As we talked, firelight shone on the king's ring. Though the countess wore the ring, I could see the serpent feigning sleep beneath the tree. Already I felt the kingly power that James had breathed upon it.

Countess Diana, aware that I was absorbed by the ring, held out her plump hand. "How beautiful," she said, turning it on her finger. "The gold-chased band, the green stone, which I deem to be an emerald."

"A most lovely ring," I said offhandedly, in no way letting her know that I was determined to have it back. That it had suddenly changed my life!

Four

The day before the masque, King James, true to his promise, arrived at Foxcroft. His cavalcade stretched for more than a mile, from Dudley Woods to Foxcroft Castle. He brought good weather, a green silk pavilion, enough victuals to fuel an army, more than fifty retainers, dozens of lordly guests, and others of note.

From my tower, as the long cavalcade passed, I searched for Anthony Foxcroft. He was not in the line of horsemen. And when I did not see him among those who stepped out of the coaches, I hurried to Countess Diana with the bad news.

I found her in the Great Arcade, beside the fish pool, feeding carp with her gloved hands. She received the news calmly.

"If by chance you meet the king, do not question him about Anthony. He dislikes questions very much."

We were surprised by the appearance of Robert Carr, who came to announce that the king had gone off on a hunt but had wished to convey his greetings to the countess.

I had seen him riding in light armor, dust-covered, beside the king. He had changed his attire and now wore a red doublet with white ruffs and meshed black stockings. His

26

auburn hair was curled in wavy locks. His skin glowed with health. Conveniently at his right hand he carried a thin jeweled case sheathing a Spanish dagger.

He was a splendid-looking creature. Yet I noticed at once that there lurked in his glance a hint of discomfort. He was worried. He was burdened by some dark thought.

As soon as Carr had turned stiffly on his heel and left us, I remarked on his manner. The countess had also noticed that he was ill at ease.

"I take it," she said, "that Anthony has been freed, against Carr's wishes, and is on his way. I hope something delays him—a pretty face or a game of cards—until Carr and the king have gone. Otherwise, I fear a troublesome time."

Anthony arrived toward the end of dinner. The countess had borrowed a dozen deer from our neighbor, the duchess of Wythe, and had set them loose in the woods, so when the king trotted back from his hunt he brought with him four fat stags, which were roasted over the fire pit. Royal servants in gold livery served them on trestles.

Having no taste for food, I found a place near the pavilion's only door, two embroidered flaps attended by guards, and waited. Anthony came during a drinking song, while horns brayed and all the men were on their feet. He parted the curtains and took in the scene with one quick glance. Carr stood beside the king.

A companion at Anthony's shoulder whispered, "There he is, in the red doublet."

"I see," Anthony said. "Who could miss him? Six feet tall, wrapped in a red, fur-trimmed doublet, a diamond sparkling in his ear."

"Now is the time to have a word with him," the companion whispered, "calmly, yet so all may hear."

"Yes, my friend. The time is right. I'll speak politely yet to the point," Anthony said.

I was on my feet at once. " 'Tis not the time," I said, putting out my hand to hold him back.

He was surprised, not having seen me. He stepped back as if at an enemy's touch.

" 'Tis foolish to come here at this moment," I said. "You're free by the good will of His Majesty. Don't embarrass him by words with Carr of any kind, polite or impolite."

Parting the curtains, I shoved him not so gently, past a throng of attendants, away from the pavilion. He turned an astounded gaze upon me.

"You can't be Serena Lynn," he said, lifting my chin, pushing my head from side to side. "Yes, you are, but what has come upon you? You act like a scullery wench."

"Nothing," I said. "I am just glad to see you and determined. Determined to see that you not quarrel with Robert Carr."

Reluctantly, he picked me up and kissed me, then set me down with a thump. "You have no idea what I've been through," he said in a strained voice that was not his at all. "A journey through hell that you can scarcely imagine. My guide, Robert Carr, smilingly at hand throughout, pouring in my ear a stream of admonitions and ill-concealed threats, as though he were the king himself."

There was a starry sky above us and the sound of night birds in the trees. The last thing I wanted to hear in all this world was an account of his troubles with Robert Carr, but doggedly he went on.

"The Tower," he said, "is not a tower. It's a cave, albeit paneled in wood. The slanting roof crouches, parts of it so low you dare not stand straight, the rest a menacing shadow hanging above your head. It has no furniture, not a chair or a bench. The bare walls catch every sound, distort and throw it back at you in trailing echoes. Carr's words as he

stood at the door and bade me enter were like stones tossed
into a pit."

Anthony no longer spoke in a strained voice. It was the
voice of an angry youth mindlessly bent, whatever the cost,
upon revenge.

"It was a place of doom I stepped into at Carr's request.
The floor beneath my feet seemed slippery with the tears
and blood of a thousand helpless souls, so yielding that I
found it difficult to walk.

"'Step in,' Robert Carr urged me. 'It's warmer within
than without and more friendly than you would ever believe.
There are even those, the stubborn ones, who wish to return
and often do.'"

The singing and the bleat of horns had stopped. The
pavilion was quiet for a time. I thought I heard the king's
thin voice, then the singing began again.

"A clutch of candles burned in tall iron holders,"
Anthony said, "casting their yellow light upon the Tower's
centerpiece, a wooden rack much like those we use here at
Foxcroft for hanging clothes, though of larger dimensions.
And, it has the means by which you can be strapped upon it
securely, with a cunning system of screws to twist and turn
and pull you slowly apart.

"I stared at the contraption, certain that Carr had no
thought of using it upon me. I was there to be frightened,
humiliated, given a taste of his power.

"My eyes having grown accustomed to the dim light, I
made out two men in the shadows, alertly watching. At my
side Robert Carr said, 'The rack is old. Carpenters are
working on a new one. It's more elegant, the frame
fashioned of pearwood, the straps brass-studded and made
of cordovan. When you come again, you will also find
brighter lanterns to light your way. The Tower is a bit
gloomy now, don't you think?'

"'Yes, and it smells,' I said. 'But what can you do about

that, since the stones reek of pain and blood? You would need to gather new stones, build a new Tower.' "

Anthony finished his story with a laugh. He seemed to think he had bested Robert Carr.

"You're tilting with a dangerous man," I said. "He sees in you a rival for the king's affection. Remember how James made over you on his visits to Covington."

"I remember well."

" 'Tis better not to remember. Forget those days and stay away as best you can from both while they're here."

"I take your words for wisdom."

I believed him as I led the way along the dark path, away from the pavilion. No, it was not a belief that I held to, only a hope.

Five

The masque was presented the next evening, though it had been planned for the afternoon. The king and Robert Carr had gone hunting at dawn and hadn't returned until dark. It was just as well. The day was sweltering hot. A sultry wind blew from the marshes and the sun beat down from a coppery sky.

Countess Diana did well with the story of Drake's raid upon the coast of Spain. Two fighting ships, one Spanish, one English, she had placed facing each other in the meadow. The hulls were made of cloth, the cannon of wood, painted black. But from the terrace, where her guests would gather, the ships had the look of two furious antagonists, ready to sink each other with one mighty blast. The blast she had placed in her son's charge, no doubt to keep his mind from dwelling upon Robert Carr.

Although the king was in a sullen mood upon his arrival, having had poor luck on the hunt, Countess Diana asked him to open the masque with a few words about the starving colony in Virginia. She pressed him to remind the lords and ladies that seven ships and two pinnaces lay at anchor in Plymouth Bay, unable to sail because half of them were empty, and that, while they had lunched upon capon, calf's head with green sauce and bacon, herring pie and Florentine tarts, the starving settlers in Jamestown—Englishmen every one—supped on bowls of watery gruel, if at all.

The king had no blood on him, as a result of the poor hunt. But his clothes were in disarray and he was sweating. Instead of talking about the settlers' plight, he dove ahead to the time when the colony would be successful, returning great riches to the mother country.

"But the riches will not come from the growing of tobacco," he warned. "This I forbid. Smoking is a custom loathsome to the eye, hateful to the nose, harmful to the brain, dangerous to the lungs, and in the black, stinking fume thereof, nearest resembling the horrible Stygian smoke of the pit that is bottomless. Seven thousand tobacconists ply their trade in London, where men puff upon clay pipes, infecting themselves and the air. I may lock the door of every one!"

It was not a speech that encouraged those who planned to make a fortune growing tobacco to buy shares in the company of Adventurers and Planters of the City of London for the First Colony of Virginia.

Captain John Smith more than made up for what the king had lost. He had just come back from Virginia, suffering from a bad powder burn, and should have been in bed, yet he came down all the way from London. Walking with difficulty—a powder flask had exploded in his lap—he was helped to the terrace and held while he spoke.

In a stout voice, he described the conditions at Jamestown the day he left. "There's more semblance of order among the colonists than when I arrived in 1607," he said. "Less feuding with the Indians, brighter prospects for the English investor who wishes to enhance his funds. To purchase a share in the Virginia Company, I truly believe, is to purchase a share in the future of England."

Someone called out to ask if Jamestown was still a dumping ground for murderers, thieves, idle persons, the disinherited, a sink crammed with the floating scum of the world.

Captain Smith did not answer, but he went on speaking for half an hour, though his voice fell to a whisper. When he finished, he called me over, and in a grand gesture before all those assembled, took out his purse and bought two shares in the Virginia Company.

He put a light hand upon my shoulder. "I understand that more men have signed for the voyage than can be accommodated. A goodly number of women also. But more are needed. Would it be—may I ask if you could be persuaded to grace our endeavors with your presence?"

Good heavens above! The very idea of four thousand miles in a bobbing ship, bound for a place, whatever Captain Smith said, where people lived on gruel, died from fever and Indian arrows, made my stomach lurch. Yet I did not recoil but managed a smile and a promise to give his suggestion thought.

"You would be an addition in Virginia," he said through the silky brown beard that covered most of his mouth. "Most of the women who have signed to go out are a dour lot. You seem quite the contrary. Lighthearted, yet in your eyes I discern a look that might well daunt the devil. You remind me of a dear friend I had in Jamestown. She was frolicsome, too. She liked to turn cartwheels and swing from trees. Do you?"

I shook my head.

"Her name is Pocahontas. It means mischievous, playful, frolicsome. She's the favorite daughter of Chief Powhatan. Once, in a friendly mood, I went to parley with him but was seized and my head placed upon the killing stone. Wildly, Pocahontas threw herself upon me and thus saved my life."

"She must have been in love."

"She was, and when time went on, I with her."

"But you didn't marry?"

"No, she was very young, a mere child. I loved her as a daughter."

He sounded much like Anthony Foxcroft, who thought of me, who treated me, as if I too were a mere starry-eyed child, someone too young to know her mind.

He passed a hand across his eyes. "I send my love to her with each ship that sails for Jamestown."

There were short pieces on the zither, then bagpipes in honor of the Scottish-born king. Between pieces, loud talk came from the English ship where Anthony was captain, and thither I saw servants dodging through the bushes with mugs of sparkling wine.

The countess had sent a coach to Stratford for William Shakespeare, and he had come, bringing his daughter Judith, a handsome woman with yellow curls, and his son, Hamnet. To music on the viol, he recited a tearful monologue composed by Countess Diana, which may be the reason his tongue tripped now and again. Only when he reached the part where the Spanish king, upon learning of Drake's victories, shut himself away and no one dared speak to him did the great poet seem at ease.

I am not certain, but I think he wrote this part himself. The words, "Seas incarnadine, where sailors' eyes were plucked by ravening sharks," sounded more like Shakespeare than Diana Foxcroft.

The battle between the ships of England and Spain was a disappointment. There were two feeble shots from each, then for some reason a cloud of black smoke rose from the scene and the cloth ships disappeared in flames. It was just as well. No one was hurt in the explosion and by now the guests were quite hungry.

As I left the terrace the king sought me out. He had managed to change from his hunting attire and now wore a white and black doublet and black silk stockings with white butterflies woven into them. Diamonds sparkled on his chest and his fingers.

Since the countess had the serpent ring, I wisely wore gloves because I knew he would look for the circlet, which he did.

Robert Carr, at his side, wished to know if I still had shares to sell. I had three, and he bought one of them. The king bought the other two.

The king said, "Captain John Smith, after his eloquent speech, went about among the ladies and some of the maids, trying to enlist them in the Jamestown project. Did he light on you?"

"Yes, Your Majesty."

"What did you say?"

"I thanked him."

"Splendid. We need you at court. The queen admires your handwriting—I showed her the invitation. She desires you as a secretary. You will help with her correspondence and numerous jottings. What do you say, young lady?"

"I am speechless, sire!"

"When can you be with us? In two days' time?"

"I'll have to speak to Countess Diana."

"There's nothing to speak about," Robert Carr said. " 'Tis a command you've received. Kingly commands are not dithered over. Be ready for the day after tomorrow. The king will hunt until noon. Be packed by then. You may bring as many things as you wish."

"I haven't much to bring."

"Bring yourself," the king said. "I'll see to the rest."

But it was not Countess Diana I wanted to speak to. To have a friend at court, a royal secretary, would please her mightily. Anthony Foxcroft was free. I could never leave him, not even to be the queen of England. I hurried into the arcade, where I had caught sight of Anthony, to persuade him somehow to come to London with me.

Six

The Great Arcade is Countess Diana's sweet conceit, her proudest jewel. It's shaped like two lofty crescents with fountains between. Artificial trees—oranges and lemon, pomegranate and mimosa—line the walks. Stuffed birds of all colors from lands as far away as Morocco inhabit the trees and sing songs when golden cords are pulled. In daylight a sun shines down through fleecy clouds. At night a moon, a different one each night, glides across the sky and stars twinkle.

Anthony was standing beside one of the fountains, a hand on his hip, the other on the hilt of his dagger. He said something to Robert Carr, who stood beside him, in a soft voice that I couldn't hear.

I distinctly heard Carr say, in a loud, taunting voice, "You made an awful mess with the battle scene. You look like a chimney sweep."

Anthony's face was smudged from the explosion. He did look like a chimney sweep.

"It's a great wonder," Robert Carr said, "that you didn't blow yourself up, as well as me and the king. I mustn't find fault, though. Powder's an unbroken horse. It requires a strong grip and two firm hands."

The moon glided directly above our heads. Silver light fell upon us, but only for a moment or two at most. In that brief time, it all happened. I saw it unclearly, yet I saw the knife in Anthony's hand dart toward Robert Carr, who was moving away. I saw Carr's body servant slip between the two like a shadow.

There wasn't a sound, not a gasp. The two men were staring at each other. The servant lay sprawled between them, legs hanging over the rim of the fountain, his blood staining the water.

White clouds moved slowly across the moon. I heard the clatter of a knife upon the stones. I heard the soft grinding of the wooden cogs that moved the heavens above me. I saw Anthony bend low over the servant and touch his forehead. Behind me I heard Countess Diana's voice, then a scream—hers or a scream from someone else.

In the darkness that had settled upon the room, now lit by only a few scattered candles, I led Anthony away. Past men who were running toward the fountain, past a knot of fluttering women, through a lane of trees where we knocked off waxen fruit in our flight, up the winding stairs. As I started to close the tower door, Countess Diana pushed it open and stepped into the room.

Anthony had gone to the window, the one that looked down upon the black water of the river. He whirled around at his mother's voice.

"You're thinking of France," she said. "But you cannot flee to France. Carr, or the king himself, will have you back ere your feet touch the coast."

Anthony's face was white. "The wrong man, the wrong man!" he said through colorless lips.

"Waste no time upon the servant's life. Give thought to

your own," his mother said. "You don't have days or hours
to do so. Minutes, at most."

Anthony again looked down upon the river, toward the
coast of France, which in the dark night he could not see.

"Give up France," the countess said. " 'Tis the same as
fleeing straight to London and back to the Tower."

"Ireland?" he said. "I could go to Ireland. The Irish are
so busy killing each other they'd never take note of me."

"With your blue eyes, lanky black hair, and white, white
skin, they might mistake you for an Irishman," she said.
"Your grandfather was an Irishman, you know."

Anthony was silent. He lifted his shoulders in a defiant
shrug. For an awful moment I feared that he had decided not
to run from Robert Carr. Wrapped in one of his romantic
dreams, he had chosen death instead of a chance to escape.

I opened the door and listened. Lively sounds of dancing
welled up from below. They did not deceive me. The king
might be tripping across the floor, but not Robert Carr.
Listening to the revelry I was struck by an improbable
thought. I closed the door and locked it with the double
bolt.

Anthony glanced at me. "You're excited," he said. "You
must have heard something."

"Only sweet music and dancing, but I've had a thought.
A wild one. We have sold the shares necessary to provision
all seven ships. They'll be sailing for Jamestown in two
weeks or sooner. You're a strong man, young and adventurous. The countess can get a place for you, even though the
boats are full."

" 'Tis something to think on," the countess said casually.

I knew her. She was pretending. She'd thought of
Jamestown long before I had. She was determined to send
Anthony to the New World. Who better to watch over her
vast properties than her own son!

Anthony brightened. "I hear the savages out there have

mountains of gold. It is said they eat from gold plates and wear gold sandals with which they tread floors paved with gold."

"I have heard this," I said, opening the door again.

"Simple people, too," Anthony said. "With courage and a little luck, a man could become an emperor in the New World."

"What do you hear?" he asked me.

"The dancing has stopped. Drums and fifes are playing a mournful song. A death march from the crusades, I think."

"A timely thought," he said.

"Selected, no doubt, by Robert Carr and meant for your ears," his mother said.

"When he comes, give him my fair tidings," Anthony said. He kissed his mother and lifted me from my feet. "Thank him for the thoughtful warning."

Two stairways led down from the tower, one into the Great Arcade, the other, by a series of secret windings, to a postern hidden in the trees. Anthony took the secret path.

While we stood in the doorway, guards in ribbons and fancy armor came, wanting to know if we were hiding Anthony Foxcroft. When the countess told them that she knew nothing of his whereabouts, they brushed past us and ransacked the tower, much to her disgust.

They looked in the small bed, under the bed, in the clothespress, and behind the draperies. A wicker chest, which I had planned to use for my journey to court, scarcely large enough to hide a midget, was locked. They demanded the key, opened the chest, and departed, clambering down the stairs to search the next floor.

At Countess Diana's bidding, I closed the door and snuffed the candles. In the dark I followed her to the south window, which had a view of the stable. A half-moon shone overhead, and by its light, after what seemed a very long time, we saw Anthony ride out and take the road that led to Wentworth Village.

The countess clasped me to her bosom and let out a grievous moan. But most of her grief, I believed, was for show. She was really glad her son was bound for Jamestown. Not only would it put him beyond Carr's reach, but it would offer him an exciting life not to be found at Foxcroft and a golden chance to enrich himself. Above all, he could keep a watchful eye upon the lands, rivers, and meadows she owned in the shining wilderness of Virginia. Yes, she was happy to see him go. It was my heart that was breaking.

The king was off hunting the next day from dawn until noon. At noon he sent for me. I found him in the pavilion, seated in a canopied chair, picking at a plate of roasted duck, his long, blood-stained cuffs rolled back. I stood for a while before he looked up; when he did, his glance was fixed upon my forehead.

"The mark is still there," he said, "so I shan't need to make another one. Has it protected you well?"

"Oh, yes, Your Majesty, very well," I said, though no one could see the mark but the king and me.

He fastened me with his sharpest look. I expected him to ask about the happening of yesterday night—what I knew, where Anthony was hiding himself. Instead, he asked about the serpent ring.

"You aren't wearing it, young lady. Why not?"

I gathered my wits and sought an answer. But what could I say save the truth?

"Countess Diana has it."

"Has it?"

I glimpsed a ray of hope. "She's keeping the ring for special times. It's so priceless she's afraid I'll lose it."

" 'Tis to be worn. 'Tis a part of you, like your hand, like your heart. God gave it to me, King James of England, His princely voice, His holy presence here on earth. 'Tis a sacred ring, therefore. Wear it now and all times, even when you sleep."

He called a guard and sent him posthaste with instructions to retrieve the ring and not to return without it.

"Have you gathered your things? Your magical pens?" he asked me. "We move at noon, soon after the hunt. Don't bother with clothes. Wear what you wear now. You'll be dressed properly, in courtly fashion, when you reach London."

He put down his knife, shoved the untouched duck away, and then described the life I would be introduced to. It was a glowing picture he painted—the eminent men, the lords and ladies I would meet, the dances, the courtly fetes I would attend.

"Sometime," he said, "and may God delay the day, a worthy knight will claim you."

I followed his every word. I smiled, I nodded, made little signs of pleasure, was charmed beyond the powers of speech. Yet withal, every second of the time my deepest thoughts never strayed once from Anthony Foxcroft.

The servant came back, red-faced, with the ring. His Majesty rose and in reverent silence placed it on my finger. Then he glanced at my forehead. Satisfied with what he saw, he dismissed me with a smile.

That night, as the castle slept under a half-moon, I packed my best clothes and made my way to the stables. A horse I had ridden before, which was slow-footed yet reliable, followed me through the trees until I was out of hearing. After climbing to his back, I plodded down the road past Wentworth, past Selby, toward the distant town of Plymouth.

At sunrise, reaching Darnley Village, I stopped at a tavern and slept till midmorning. When I had quickly breakfasted and was about to start off in a slanting rain, the tavernkeeper advised me not to leave. There were highway-men on the road ahead.

"Five travelers were robbed last night," he said. "They all lost their purses. One lost his life. It's foolish, miss, to go farther."

I thanked him kindly and rode off in the rain, clenching the serpent ring, my guardian, my protection against all harm.

Seven

I arrived in Plymouth after nine days and nights on muddy roads in wind and rain. I rode by post horses part of the time, having little in my purse and my own horse having given out. I'd had to borrow two pounds from Countess Diana, leaving a note with a promise to return the money.

Yet nothing of this ordeal mattered. The fleet had not sailed. The ships lay at anchor in the calm waters of Plymouth Bay, flags flying from their masts, decks aswarm with settlers. And as I rode up the cobbled street I saw Anthony Foxcroft standing at the door of the White Lamb Tavern in conversation with a group of men.

Not an hour had passed since the day I left home that I hadn't worried about him. Had he changed his mind and gone off to hide himself in France? Had he met with some horrible accident? Had Robert Carr set guards on his trail and arrested him? But, miracle of miracles, there he stood in a sky-blue doublet and a feathered cap, his long hair shining in the bright sun.

I rode past him up the cobbled street and gave over my hired horse to the post rider who had accompanied me the last leg of the journey. In my heavy cloak, with my fur hood pulled down, I walked back to the tavern, thinking to slip inside unnoticed—my boots were muddy, my clothes travel-stained, and I hadn't touched water in days—but while his listeners waited for him to go on with something he was saying, Anthony stopped and called out to me.

"You took your time, Serena, dear. I looked for you days ago."

My cheeks flamed. I was embarrassed by his greeting but not astounded. He certainly knew that wherever he went, be in France or Ireland or the Low Countries, I would follow him. Since that far day, the very day I had fallen in love with him, when had he ever doubted his power over me?

"The nag you just rode down the street," he went on, "is fit only for crows. You must have hired a stable full of crow baits, for they took most of a fortnight to get you here. Another day and you'd have been too late. The fleet sails in the morning early."

I said nothing in reply. I turned away and left him in the street, paid for a room in the tavern with the last of my money, ordered two tubs of hot water and a maid to scrub me, fell asleep in the second tub, and was awakened at nightfall by word that a gentleman from one of the ships bound for Jamestown wished to see me.

A tall, stooped, very thin young man with yellowish skin and fiery eyes was waiting in the common room, pacing up and down, his bony hands behind his back. He gave me a sharp look as I came down the stairs. Something about me—my smile, the pink satin slippers, the red ribbons in my hair—caused him to purse his lips. He continued his pacing until I boldly introduced myself, suspecting that he was the gentleman who wished to talk to me.

He bowed stiffly and said that he was Richard Bucke, clergyman on the ship *Sea Venture*. "I understand from

Anthony Foxcroft that you wish to join us on our voyage to the New World."

"This is my intention."

" 'Tis noble of you, yes, noble, but I wonder if you have given thought to the hardships you'll encounter on shipboard and in the New World?"

He spoke slowly, in a reverent voice, but eyed me suspiciously the while, still wondering, as far as I could tell, if I might turn out to be a hindrance rather than a help.

"Have you had, by chance, experience on a farm, with animals, crops, and such?"

"Oh, yes," I said, determined that the *Sea Venture* would never, never sail without me. "Foxcroft, where I come from, is a vast estate. I was born at Foxcroft. I grew up among horses and cows."

The Reverend Bucke looked at my hands, the ring on my finger. He pursed his lips again. He was about to say that there was no room for me on the *Sea Venture*.

I took off the ring. "If you'll look inside the band," I said, "you'll find the king's crest. He gave me the ring."

"King James!" the Reverend Bucke exclaimed. I nodded.

"Why, pray tell?"

"He admires my writing. He has asked me to come to London to write letters for the queen. But I came here, instead, to talk to you."

The Reverend Bucke smiled. He gave back the ring. Certainly, by some kingly magic, it had changed his mind about me.

"I'll need to write letters whilst in Jamestown," he said. "Perhaps you can be of help. I write a hand scarcely to be read by anyone, even myself."

"And also, sir, I can help you write down your sermons. You will give many, I am sure."

"Two every day will be the order of things. But I do not write sermons down. They fly to my tongue like birds."

From his slashed brown doublet he fished a long listing, and I put my name to a contract.

"*Sea Venture* sails before noon tomorrow," he said. "Be on the quay at dawn. Bring only necessities—only what you can comfortably carry. We'll have one hundred and forty-nine aboard, one hundred and fifty counting you. Space is limited."

Space was more than limited. Soon after dawn I was taken aboard the *Sea Venture*, to the afterdeck and down a few narrow steps into a dungeon where the roof was so low I had to stoop. I was given a space that measured no more than a stride in width and two strides in length. Not a bed or a bunk, mind you, but a sleeping place on the bare floor.

There was no one in the dungeon. Everyone was on deck in the fresh air—everyone save Anthony Foxcroft. For a few awful, tormenting hours he was nowhere to be seen. I'd have paced the deck if that were possible, but we were standing shoulder to shoulder in a place no larger than a pigpen. Somebody's beard was scraping my cheek.

Noon came. He was not in sight. Could the king's guards have captured him? I thought of going ashore, swimming ashore if need be. Then, as trumpets sounded from each of the seven ships and echoed across the bay, he appeared on the quay.

Taking his time, he sauntered down the steps, his black, wide-brimmed hat cocked on the side of his head, got into a waiting longboat, and was rowed to the ship. He came up the ladder, calling my name. He called thrice in a ringing voice. I did not answer.

"Where are you?" he shouted, alarmed, elbowing his way along the crowded deck.

I took off my hat and waved. He raised his sword and waved back. I heard him say, "You have no idea what you're . . ." He said more that I couldn't hear. Chains rattled, sails flapped, people shouted.

There were no waves in Plymouth Harbor, but the ship rocked anyway, gently up and down, back and forth. My stomach began to rock, too. I felt myself grow pale. For a fleeting moment I thought of London and King James, of the life I might have led.

Anthony grasped my arm. He led me to the rail and told me to breathe out when the ship rose up and to breathe in when the ship sank down. In this way, he said, I would feel as though the ship weren't moving at all.

I did as I was told and felt somewhat better. At last I saw White Lamb Tavern, the cobbled streets, the tumbled, slant-roofed houses, slowly disappear. And behind us six other ships followed along in a line, like six fat ducks on a pond. Farther back, trailing along like goslings, were two little boats, pinnaces, with fluttering sails.

The sun was bright on the water—too bright—and the Reverend Bucke was halfway up a mast, giving the first of his many sermons in a powerful voice. My head spun and my stomach took a twisting turn.

Eight

I was seasick for a day and a night, flat on my back on the hard floor. Anthony brought me bowls of turnip soup and the Reverend Bucke tried to comfort me with pious talk about how noble I was to be going out to help the starving people of Jamestown. I was too sick to eat the soup or to care if the ship reached Virginia or hit a rock and sank.

The second day I felt better. Much better, when the ship put in at Falmouth, not far from Plymouth, and anchored for days in the calmest of waters, while it took on eight horses and a dozen pigs.

Just when we were ready to leave, as the sails were unfurled and the dripping anchors brought in, a boatload of men nosed out of the fog. Someone in a scarlet cloak cupped his hands and shouted to us. He wanted the ship to wait, but the sails were full and we were moving.

A sailor threw him a rope, which he grasped, and he was hauled on deck. The boatload of men, shaking their fists and howling insults, disappeared in the fog.

The man in the scarlet cloak was on the ship no more than a second when he asked in a ringing voice for the fleet's commander, made his way over the crowded deck, flew up its ladder to the Great Cabin, and burst in upon Admiral Somers.

We could hear him shouting through the open door. He was John Fitzhugh, captain of the king's guards, sent by the king to arrest Anthony Foxcroft and to bring him forthwith to the Tower and justice.

Anthony and I were standing at the rail, close to the Great Cabin, but someone shut the door and we heard nothing else. It was a terrible moment. If Admiral Somers decided to turn back, Anthony would be given over to the captain of the guards and taken off the ship.

Anthony always carried a dagger. He had his hand on it now. But what could he do with it? If the ship turned back, it would be of no use to him. There was no way he could ever withstand a dozen armed guards.

We waited in silence. We rounded a low headland. This was the moment the admiral could change course and return to Falmouth. A strong wind struck us and put the ship on its beam. The door of the Great Cabin swung open. Admiral Somers stood looking back at the town, at the men in the rigging ready to trim sail.

I do not know whether it was because he had added the hours it would require to put Anthony ashore to the earlier delays and the confusion it would cause among the ships in our wake or because he simply didn't believe John Fitzhugh, but his decision came quickly. He turned, closed the door behind him, and let us sail south, into the open sea.

Fitzhugh remained on board, and that night, while we were eating our supper, the admiral sent for Anthony.

Anthony didn't come back, though I waited for hours.

When I came on deck in the morning, the Reverend Bucke said that Admiral Somers wished a word with me. It seemed that Bucke had informed the admiral about my friendship with King James.

We climbed the steep ladder to the sterncastle, to the gilded door of the Great Cabin, and went into a paneled room of carved beams and Persian rugs. Admiral Somers sat at a desk under the stern window, where he had a view of the eight ships sailing along behind us. He was stout and pink-cheeked, and he spoke briskly.

"When last did you see His Majesty?" he asked me.

"Less than two weeks ago, sir, at Foxcroft where I live."

"I trust he was in good health."

"Excellent health, sir. And he's very active in hunting."

Admiral Somers appraised me with a glance. I was wearing my best dress—a trim, white ruff with a sky-blue skirt open down the front to reveal a crocus-colored petticoat. It was a pretty dress. Anthony liked it and had complimented me on it.

"Where do you sleep, young lady?" he asked.

"Below in the rear," I replied, then stopped. Tired of lubberly talk, Anthony had told me that what I called the front of the ship was not the front, but the bow, and the rear was not the rear, but the stern. I corrected myself, which pleased the admiral, and said, "Below in the stern, sir, next to the rudder."

"Are you comfortable there?"

"No, sir. I am very uncomfortable. I am also worried. I have another friend, one besides King James. His name is Anthony Foxcroft and he has disappeared. I haven't seen him since yesterday evening. Where could he be?"

The admiral stiffened in his chair. "He's locked away. The king has sent for him. Something about a murder."

"It wasn't murder," I said. "I was there and saw it."

"Saw what?"

I took my time and told him exactly what I had seen, how the quarrel had begun and how it had ended. "It was Robert Carr's fault," I said. "And I am sure that the king didn't send for Anthony. Rather, it was Carr who sent for him— Robert Carr, his present favorite."

The admiral looked at the carved figures on the ceiling, at the ships in our wake, everywhere but at me.

"Anthony hasn't been seen since yesterday," I said. "Where is he? I must know, sir."

The admiral pointed to a small door in the paneled wall. It led, I discovered later, to a cubbyhole near the rudder, reached by the Great Cabin.

Admiral Somers smiled. "I have a surprise for you," he said, and he called an aide who showed me a cabin in an adjoining passageway.

"Do you like your new quarters?" he asked when I came back. "It's small but well appointed."

"Oh, yes. Very much."

The next morning I found my way through the small door Admiral Somers had pointed out to the cubbyhole near the rudder, where Anthony was locked behind a door with a small iron grill. It was too high for me to see through, and the noise of the rudder and the swishing seas was so loud that I had to shout Anthony's name three times before he heard me.

"I've talked to Admiral Somers," I shouted to him.

"What did he say?" Anthony shouted back.

"Nothing. But I'll talk to him again."

"Do. 'Tis an awful place they have here. I can barely turn around."

"I'll talk to Admiral Somers today."

"Good."

And that was all we said to each other.

I talked to Admiral Somers that day, but he was pleasantly evasive, more concerned about me than he was about Anthony. Once more he asked if I liked my cabin.

"Oh, yes, very much, sir," I replied, as I had the day before when he had asked me the same question.

And I did like it. It had a hammock, two leather buckets, and a small window. Besides, it was high above the commotion below—squealing pigs, neighing horses, and the incessant chatter of more than a hundred settlers cooped up like so many chickens.

I saw many things from my window during those bitter times when I was allowed to see Anthony only a few minutes of each day. Out of Falmouth, seas began to run. The captain of our ship, Christopher Newport, was forced to cut the rope fastened to the *Virginia*, the pinnace we were towing. I watched her turn about in the towering waves and head back to England.

Days later, early in the morning, I heard the gunports clang open, and I saw through the window two strange ships on the horizon. Word came from Captain Newport that they were Spanish privateers. If they sailed toward us, the ship's bell would ring three times, a signal for all the women to gather below decks. But the bells didn't ring. The privateers had compared their strength to ours.

On the thirty-first day, under a scorching sun, word came that plague had broken out in the *Lion* and the *Blessing*, two of the ships sailing in our wake. I saw bodies, wrapped in canvas, dropped into the sea. Rumor was that thirty-two had died during the hot weather, nearly half of them women and children.

The weather grew mild, the waves glassy as they followed us along. We were now well past the bulge of Africa and the Canary Islands, on the same route Christopher Columbus had taken more than a hundred years before, under the same sun and stars, driven by the same gentle winds.

It was the first time since we left Falmouth that the settlers were happy. Evenings they gathered on the main deck (the waist, as it was called), sang songs of home, and danced to flutes and drums. One night John Fitzhugh, Carr's man, recited a love poem he had written. I had avoided him throughout the voyage, and I did then as he received the plaudits of the crowd and came lumbering up—he was the size of a stump—to receive mine.

The mild weather did not last. Captain Newport changed course and we sailed north by west. The winds were confused, now blowing from the south, now from the east, at times not blowing at all. The sun was hot, but at night we saw no stars in the heavens. The sailors went about the deck, closing the open hatches, battening them down with canvas to keep out running waves. We were told by Captain Newport to see that all our possessions were well fastened.

The Reverend Bucke preached sermons every morning and night. On the twenty-third of July, after a starless night, the wind dying to a whisper, he preached at noon. Standing against the mizzenmast with everyone gathered around him, he mopped his brow and offered the following prayer:

> *O Eternal God, who alone spreadest out the heavens and rulest the raging of the sea, we commend to Thy almighty protection Thy servants for whose preservation on the great deep our prayers are desired. Guard them, we beseech Thee, from the dangers of the sea and conduct them in safety to their haven in the New World.*

With fearful thoughts people gazed at the yellow sky, at the sea, which was smooth as a woodland pond, at the sails hanging limp in the quiet air. But every one of us, I do believe, welcomed a change in the weather, even a storm.

After sixty long days under a scorching sun, the drinking water turned brackish. The sea biscuits, one of our staple foods, had gathered weevils. Half of the turnips, another of our staples, shriveled, and the rest went rotten. The whole ship stank. Noisome privies, rancid food, smoke from the rushlights, the smell of unwashed bodies, all combined in one powerful stench that clogged the nostrils and assailed the stomach.

In the silence that followed the Reverend Richard Bucke's prayer, I climbed the ladder and spoke to Admiral Somers.

"When the storm comes," I said, "please do not forget that Anthony Foxcroft is locked away in a cubbyhole."

"The safest place," the admiral said. "The very best. Foxcroft will be the last to drown."

This was gallows humor. The admiral couldn't be serious, but still it angered me. "King James is a friend of Countess Diana," I said. "He would never arrest her son for something that wasn't his fault. It's Robert Carr's arrogance, as I have said before and say again. 'Tis silly to keep Anthony confined. Where would he go if you unlocked him? Would he leave the ship and walk away?"

"You might speak to Governor Gates," the admiral said to be rid of me. Sir Thomas Gates was the appointed governor of Virginia. He had quarters in the sterncastle. He kept to himself and I had seen him only from a distance.

"I am in command of the fleet," the admiral continued, "but once we reach Virginia, which we shall do quite soon, the governor is in charge. Talk to him, Miss Lynn."

"I shall, at once." But the words were scarcely spoken when a shrieking wind fell upon the ship. I was thrown to the deck and lay there half-stunned. Yet I had enough wits about me to close my hand, to clench it tight upon the king's ring, lest it be ripped from my finger. The sterncastle door flew open, and a woman took hold of my hand and dragged me to safety. She noticed the ring.

"How did you come by it?" she asked. "Did you steal it in the dark of the moon?"

" 'Tis a gift from the king."

"Unlikely, yet the king is a generous man. My mistress owned such a ring. She found it an antidote for the dangers of this world. I trust that you have found it such."

"I have."

"And will continue to do so, though the ship sinks and everyone drowns, save you?"

I did not answer. In the light from a lamp swinging in gimbals, I saw a tall, bleak-looking woman of middle age with stringy hair and a long, thin nose that nearly met her chin—a child's version of a witch.

"I fear that the ship is doomed," she said. "What a tragedy that will be. The admiral of the fleet and the new governor of Virginia, both these splendid men chosen to look after us in the New World, both are here, cooped up in the *Sea Venture*. It is a bad beginning, something tells me."

With her long white fingers, she made a sign and raised her eyes to heaven.

"When were you born?" she asked.

"The twenty-third day of May in the year 1593."

"Which makes you a Gemini. Born at what hour?"

"I don't know."

"Probably at dusk, under the evening star. What's your name, young miss?"

"Serena Lynn."

"Poetic. Mine is Emma Swinton, which isn't such. I would not have selected it had I been asked. Names can rule your life."

The ship pitched to the fury of a south wind, but the lamp rested steady in its gimbals.

"You have recovered from your blow?" Emma Swinton asked.

"Almost, thank you."

"Is there something I can do for you?" she said at the door, ducking her head to keep from striking the oaken beams. "Are you comfortable here? Do you want for anything? I am on my way to read the stars for Governor Gates, who is a true believer in the science. I can say a word or two in your behalf." She looked down at me with a motherly eye.

I sat up straight in my bunk and grasped her hand. "Say to him that Anthony Foxcroft is not guilty of murder. 'Tis an awful mistake to hold him in durance."

"More than a mistake," Emma Swinton said. "It is most heartbreaking for you."

Nine

Tumult increased through the day, and day became a starless night, as if Jonas himself were flying through Tarshish. Lightning flashed, then night became day again.

Through my window I saw nothing but raging water. The *Virginia* had turned back to England days before, and the ships that had followed us so faithfully all the way from Plymouth were gone.

At dawn word came that sometime in the night the ship had begun to leak. Water stood knee-deep in the bilge. Alarms sounded and the ship's roster was divided into three shifts and sent below to work at the pumps. Even Mistress Horton, her maid, and some of the common women were assigned shifts.

Anthony was still locked away. Before I took my turn at the pumps, I hurried down to see him.

The bars were so close together that I couldn't reach through them. The air was so befouled that I could scarcely breathe. The shrieking of the wind, the pounding of the waves, the banging of the rudder as it swung back and forth, made it impossible to hear.

I shouted that I was doing my best to free him. He

shouted something back and made a gesture that I could not understand. Was it indifference or the opposite? I smiled and he smiled back. The alarm sounded again. I sent him a kiss and tore myself away.

Most of the men and half of the women were below by now. Only a group of gentlemen, who had never worked a day in their lives, stayed on deck. Admiral Somers coaxed them below by going down himself and taking a pump handle.

We took turns working at the three pumps, pumping one hour at a time, resting an hour, thousands of strokes in each watch. The rest of the company filled kettles, carried them aloft, and dumped the water into the sea.

Before noon the pump I was using clogged up. Water had broken into the stores, and sea biscuits were floating around the hole. A handful had been sucked up by the pump.

While it was being cleaned, I was given the task of gathering baskets of soggy biscuits. The two other pumps got clogged and had to be taken apart; yet during the day we rid the ship of more than thirty tons of water.

It was not enough. The sea still poured in.

That night our watch was sent below again. My hands were blistered and bleeding from handling the pump, so I was given a rushlight and told to search out the leak.

Twenty of us—Mistress Horton's maid, three girls I had never seen, the boatswain, coopers, and carpenters—waded in water up to our knees, up to our necks when the ship rolled, moving from bow to stern, peering at every plank we could reach, stumbling along in the darkness lit only by our candles, while the three pumps clattered and the waves pounded the ship like a drum.

We searched until noon and found neither holes nor split planks, but only a seam, no longer than my arm, where the caulking was pushed in.

The carpenters set to work on it. For some reason they

were out of oakum and had to use substitutes—strips of dried beef, pieces of bedding, and torn dresses. But everything they stuffed in the crack came out.

At nightfall the wind died away. The Reverend Bucke prayed and everyone felt better, thinking that the storm had come to an end. But soon after the ship's bell had rung for the midnight watch, as I lay awake in pain from my blistered hands, I heard scurrying footsteps.

I got up and went down the passage to the sterncastle. Sailors were on deck furling all the sails they had run up at dusk except a small one in the bow, which was used to steady the ship. I wondered that they were taking in the sails, for there was no wind and the sea was calm.

I was aware of a light on the mainmast, on its very tip where no light could possibly be. It looked like a small, trembling star.

Someone on the deck below called out, "St. Elmo's fire."

"St. Elmo?" I called back. "Who is that?"

"All I know about is the fire. If you see fire like that it means a storm's coming."

"The storm has come already."

"A bigger storm will come, maybe a hurricane."

While we talked, the star sparkling in the masthead became two stars.

"If the lights move down the rigging, it means fair weather," the man said. "If they go up, it means foul weather."

As we talked, the two stars flew to the foremast and sat there, giving off a spectral glow. Then they flew from mast to mast, then hovered above us like two frightened birds.

"A bad sign," the man said. "I have seen it before. I am the only one saved from the bark *Louisa*. Dad and I were homeward bound when we hit a noisome gale. We saw the fire playing about the rigging just like that. My dad said, 'If we get out of here, I don't want you sailing in the bark again.' when I got back to Plymouth I took my pay and left. My father signed because he was the mate. And she went down the very next time, with all hands. So I am the only man preserved from the *Louisa*."

The man disappeared. As I went back along the passageway, I had trouble walking. The ship had taken on more water, though the pumps were still being manned.

Just before dawn I was awakened by a cannon shot. The ship was no longer sailing. She was being driven by the wind, from one side, then to the other, to the north, to the east, to the west. At times it seemed as if she were moving in circles, yet always with a dangerous slant.

To put the ship on an even keel, Captain Newport gave orders to clear out everything on her starboard side. Sailors brought up hogsheads of oil, barrels of vinegar, trunks and chests belonging to the settlers, and threw them into the sea. Mistress Horton lost two trunks and three chests. Since my cabin was at the center of the ship I lost none of my few possessions.

All through that day waves swept over the bow, flooding the deck, crashing against the heavy doors of the sterncastle. The long arm of the steering rudder, which in calm weather was managed by one man, now required the strength of six.

For fear of being swept away, the settlers huddled below. Captain Newport sent me down to help the women with children. He had ordered all the pumps stopped, since they were useless. There was meat, but no fire in the cookroom to prepare it. Water stood deep in the bilge, high above the ballast. Swarms of rats swam about, trying to flee the hold.

Toward evening, one of the women went out of her head. "We're going to drown," she screamed. "So let us close the hatches and give ourselves to God."

"Yes, to merciful God," another woman screamed.

"Amen," a man said, and started for the ladder.

I edged past him, climbed on deck, and made my way to the sterncastle. Admiral Somers and Sir Thomas Gates were arguing. They were always arguing about something: Who was in charge of the ship, the admiral of the fleet or the governor of Virginia? Where were we in the endless sea? How many days from land? From Jamestown? From anywhere?

Captain Newport was on watch. He had watched night and day since the storm struck up, though now there was little to watch. He was busy talking to a sailor. I waited.

"We are lighter to starboard with half the cargo gone," he said.

"Not light enough. We should cut the top mast and heave it over," the sailor replied.

"Let's wait for the night. The seas may moderate," Captain Newport said.

Admiral Somers spoke up. "If night ever comes."

"Poor talk," Sir Thomas Gates said. "We've not sailed this far to give up now."

"We're not giving up," the admiral said. "It's the ship that's giving up. She was never built to fight a hurricane. She's a made-over fishing smack. She used to fish for flounder in peaceful waters, off Calais."

At this moment a heavy wave lifted us high. The windows streamed with water and some of it dropped from the ceiling onto the admiral's sugar-loaf hat. He removed the hat, took a handkerchief from his sleeve, and brushed off the water. Water dropped on his bald head.

"Why do you stand with your mouth open?" the admiral asked me. "It's not Anthony Foxcroft again, I trust."

"It is, sir. He's—"

Sir Thomas Gates broke in. "Who is this Anthony Foxcroft?"

"You've heard of Foxcroft," Admiral Somers said.

"Oh, yes. Foxcroft the murderer. The one that flees the king. I haven't seen him since we left Plymouth. Where is he?"

Admiral Somers, who was busy wiping his bald head, didn't answer.

"Locked up," I said.

"Where?"

"Below. Where he'll surely drown."

"Proper punishment," Governor Gates said.

"A monstrous thing to say. You can't mean it, sir."

"But I do mean it, young lady," the governor said.

He turned his back. Admiral Somers put on his sugar-loaf hat, gave me a withering look, and dismissed me with a jerk of his thumb.

A wave, a second wave, two waves in quick succession, struck the ship. She rolled from side to side, plunged her beak deep into the towering seas, shuddered desperately as if she would never survive, and then with a great lunge rose again. Curtains of water flowed past the windows and shut off the waning day.

The three men sat in silence with their hands folded. They looked like spectors in the yellowish light, like men already dead, trapped, at the bottom of the sea. The Reverend Bucke entered with a blast of wind and he, too, looked ghostly.

I left them, went down the passage to my cabin, and slammed the door behind me. I waited for a moment, then I opened the door and listened. I heard the Reverend Bucke ask the three men to kneel, calling each by name. I heard him pray, then their response, "The Lord's name be praised."

I closed the door and by a longer way went to Anthony's cell, close upon the rudder. The rudder was lashed down by a heavy chain, and the six sailors who had manned it,

steering when the ship could be steered, lay sprawled
against the bulwarks.

A sailor asked me why I was there. When I told him, he
didn't answer. He politely pushed me through the door,
closed and bolted it, and left me standing in the wind. The
"sailor" was Fitzhugh, the king's guard.

As I hurried along the passageway, I heard the Reverend
Bucke's voice again. He was praying still, and the three
men were still responding, "The Lord's name be praised."

After a sleepless night, I dozed at dawn and awakened to
a prolonged grating sound, as if the wounded ship were
dragging herself over rocks at the bottom of the sea. I slid
from my hammock and peered out.

The window was streaked with salt, but I caught a
glimpse of the sun struggling out from a bank of pink
clouds. I heard running feet, frantic cries from the ship's
hold, and a shattering cannon shot. Then there was a short
silence followed by shouts from the sterncastle deck.

I had slept in my clothes, so I didn't need to dress. I tied
my hair in a knot and ran. Before I reached the stern ladder,
the grating sound that had awakened me grew faint and
ceased.

The ship came to a jarring halt. A prolonged shudder
crept through her planks. Then she moved on a little,
groaning as though she were trying to free herself from
some monstrous trap. Her bow nosed down at a frightening
angle, and I was thrown to the deck.

I lay quite dazed for a while, then, clambering to my feet,
I saw a stretch of still water the exact color of emeralds.
Beyond, less than a half mile away, small waves ran gently
up a beach of blinding, white sand. Beyond the beach stood
a grove of palm trees, whose fronds glittered in the sun.

Captain Newport stood on the sterncastle deck, the only
part of the ship wholly out of water, and shouted commands
to the crowd pressed against the bulwarks.

"Leave your possessions," Captain Newport said to the crowd. "Men, get yourselves ashore. The water's shallow along the reef. Women, wait for the longboat."

Mistress Horton asked him if the water was warm. The captain didn't know, so she sent her maid to find out.

William Strachey, who was the secretary-elect to Virginia, asked where we were. "It doesn't look like what I've read about Virginia." When Captain Newport was slow to answer, he said, "You're the captain and navigator. You should know."

"I do know," the captain said. "We are off Bermuda, six hundred miles east by southeast of Virginia."

"I'm bewildered," Mistress Rolfe said. "Is this an island? It seems so." Her spouse agreed.

"A lot of islands bunched together," Emma Swinton said. "If it's Bermuda, then it's a hellish place. I've read about it. Bermuda's home to haunts and devils. Its reefs are strewn with wrecks. Sailors shun its shores."

"Where would you rather be?" Captain Newport asked. "Here or on a sinking ship in the Atlantic deep?"

"Here among haunts and devils," Mistress Rolfe answered.

Emma Swinton said, "You'll come to rue these words."

Mistress Horton's maid came back to report that the water was middling hot. Mistress Horton asked the captain if he knew more about the islands than the haunts and devils and wrecks.

"Nothing more," the captain said, "except that at any moment, while you chatter, the ship may slip beneath the sea and drown us all."

Anthony Foxcroft appeared at the end of a chain held by the king's guard. Pale and drawn, encumbered by the chain, he still walked with a defiant tread. He was pushed into the longboat, and though the guard tried to shunt me away, I leaped in beside him.

Blinded in the strong sun, shading his eyes, he said, "Do I see a white beach and palm trees and water colored like emeralds?"

"You do."

"I'm not dreaming?"

"No."

"Where are we?"

"On an island. 'Tis called Bermuda."

"Bermuda? I never heard the name before. You're certain it's not heaven I see aglitter in the offing?"

The longboat slid up the beach. As he was being dragged away, I pressed the serpent ring against my heart and called, "Yes, 'tis heaven."

BOOK TWO

Bermuda

Ten

O ur ship did not slide into the sea as Captain Newport
said she might. She was wedged hard, her long beak
caught between two prongs of a coral reef. And albeit
pitched forward at an awkward slant, half of her length
lying beneath the sea, most of the things not ruined by the
storm were carried ashore that afternoon by longboat, some
on the backs of the bolder men.

There was no immediate need of shelter. The day was
windless, the shore a wide, curving stretch of white sand,
ideal for camping. The Reverend Bucke hung the ship's bell
on a palmetto tree and set it ringing.

We gathered around him gleefully—one hundred and
fifty souls—those exhausted from months cooped in a ship
meant to carry only half that many; the sick, the lame, the
injured, the homesick. We half-listened to his long sermon,
which began with the Lord's Prayer, continued to the
lessons of Jeremiah, and ended hopefully, with a plea that
we show thankfulness for being saved from certain death by
loving kindness to our neighbor.

We needed no sermon from the Reverend Bucke. Strong
men knelt and kissed the earth beneath their feet. Women

wept. Children romped on the beach. People sang until heaven resounded.

And little wonder. The endless sea, the scorching sun, the cold, maggoty food, the smells, the quarrels, the tiny ship that rolled and pitched ceaselessly, the storms, the hurricane that turned awful days into awful nights—all lay behind. Instead, as if conjured up out of a sultan's dream, was a place of sparkling seas, broad beaches, groves of palmetto trees, an island paradise.

At twilight we were camped on the beach. Driftwood fires burned brightly and three pigs were roasted on a spit. Our own surviving pigs, six of them, taken from the wreck, were hide and bones. One had wandered off into the woods and come back with three fat boars, which were tame and easily snared.

Captain Newport informed us that he had read about Juan de Bermúdez, who discovered the island a hundred years before and had left a herd of swine when he sailed off.

"The Spaniard had an eye on the future," he said. "His swine would feed upon the lush grass and multiply, furnishing ample food for the Spanish colonists yet to come. We have three of his swine already and without effort. There are more wandering around in the woods. Hundreds, thousands perhaps."

Everyone shouted at the prospect and stuffed themselves with roast pig.

After the feast I went in search of Governor Thomas Gates. I found him on the beach, about to step into the sea with Sir George Somers.

"The Reverend Bucke," I said to them, "asked us in the name of Christ to be kind to each other. To keep Anthony Foxcroft in chains is not kind. 'Tis barbarous."

Sir Thomas, a stocky man of fifty or so, broad in neck and shoulder, peered at me in dismay, edging off toward the splashing waves.

"Besides, 'tis foolish," I said. "We're marooned on an island. Our ship is wrecked beyond repair. We're six hundred miles from Jamestown. How can Anthony Foxcroft escape? He cannot walk away or swim like a fish or fly like a bird."

"I have heard this before," Sir Thomas said. "You have but a single note to your flute—Foxcroft. Foxcroft this, Foxcroft that. It's a tiresome tune you play, and I for one have become mightily sick of it."

In the fading light his black beard, which came to a point, looked like a blade, a threatening dagger.

"How's it with you, Sir George? Are you likewise sick of the name Foxcroft?"

Sir George tried the water with his big toe, mumbled, "Warm as country milk," and said, "I think that the young lady's remarks are sound. How can Foxcroft escape? No more than on the ship, I'd say. Futhermore, Fitzhugh has set a watch on him. This means men robbed from your meager force."

"Not men. Fitzhugh has assigned three of the young gentlemen to the watch: Payne, Lipscomb, and Taylor. All of little use, as you know. As for Foxcroft himself, he never condescended to clean his own quarters. He'll not be missed."

"We're without a ship," Admiral Somers said. "One will have to be built, a ship seaworthy and large enough to berth one hundred fifty people. *Sea Venture* has to be taken apart, not an easy task jammed on a reef as she is, but every plank and rib must be removed, brought ashore, and used. New timber has to be cut, sails repaired."

Governor Gates was in the water floating on his back, gazing up at the starry sky, remarking how pretty it was. He had on a pair of red drawers and his round stomach shone white. He didn't look at all like a governor, which encouraged me to tell him what I had told Admiral Somers, that Anthony had not deliberately killed anyone.

" 'Twas an accident," I said, "and the king has not sent for him. It is Robert Carr who wants him."

"The two are the same," Sir Thomas said. "They're loving twins. Injure one and you injure the other. Pinch one, the other screams."

"What's more," I said, "you treat Anthony as if he were a felon, already tried before the assizes and convicted. 'Tis wrong of you to pretend that you're both judge and jury."

The governor was playing whale, sucking in water and spouting it out. He rose at my words and jerked a finger at me.

"But I am the judge, also the jury," he shouted. "And my verdict stands. Foxcroft stays in chains."

Admiral Somers, to his knees among the small waves, reached down, took up a handful of water, and rubbed it over his chest.

"At sea," he said to Gates quietly, "you failed to recognize me as commander of the fleet. Equally now that we're on land, I hereby refuse to recognize you as the commander. You're the duly elected governor of Virginia, true. But we are not in Virginia, not yet. Perhaps we never shall be.

"We're on an island that by discovery belongs to Spain. It's our temporary home. When and if we leave here, it will be by ship, in which case I'll be in command. Until that day it's best that we divide the honors. It is my judgment that Foxcroft be allowed his freedom. Since we differ about this, let us ask Captain Newport to cast a vote and break the tie."

"That would be fair," I said, believing that Newport would agree with Somers.

The governor crept out of the sea. "Young lady," he said in a rage, "women are at work in camp, cleaning up from supper. I suggest that you hie yourself thither and join them or else I'll have you punished."

I thought it best to leave. I didn't go back to camp. I went no farther than a grove of palmetto trees, hid myself, and listened.

I heard nothing of the argument, save violent sounds, but when Gates stalked by and Admiral Somers followed at a distance, I knew that this feud, which had started the first day at sea, had not come to an end.

I ran out and overtook the admiral. "What was decided?" I asked.

"Sir Thomas insists that as governor of Virginia he's also the governor of Bermuda."

"I mean what was decided about Anthony?"

"He remains under guard."

"For how long, pray tell?"

"Until he is sent back to England."

"There's nothing you can do?"

"Little. The camp's unsettled. Sir Thomas has his followers, especially among the young gentlemen. If I make an issue of Foxcroft, it can cause trouble at a time we can ill afford trouble." He turned away and called back over his shoulder. "Be patient."

That night Sir Thomas Gates officially took command. A stiff old warrior who wanted things done at once, he divided the camp into two groups: workers and their families in one; the pampered young gentlemen, some thirty of them who during the voyage had shown a strong dislike of work, in the other.

"There's much to do," he said. "And I shall see that it's done."

Eleven

After breakfast early next day, workers were sent afield. Hunters were to bring in swine, conies, squirrels, birds—whatever they could find. Women were to gather fruits and plants; fishermen to fish the reefs.

The women came back at night with heaping baskets of cedar berries and the white hearts of palmetto tree, which proved to be flavorful. The fishermen, Admiral Somers himself casting a line, caught more than a ton of bass, barracuda, and tuna, in addition to two giant turtles so huge that just their flesh would have been sufficient for our dinner.

Birds were everywhere. White herons flew about us in flocks; sparrows tried to light on our shoulders. Hunters bagged snipe, doves, ducks, and moorhens. That first morning, two women collected sixty dozen bird eggs, hundreds of turkey eggs, sweet as butter, and nearly a thousand turtle eggs.

With two giddy boys and a stout girl, I went to dig clams in a cove just beyond our camp. We tramped the water up to our knees, finding the clams with our toes. In less than an hour we had dug five bagfuls of round ones called cockles.

72

Tom, the silliest of the boys, waded into a cave where the tide ran fast and came out shouting that he had seen a green monster.

"It's as big as a dog—a big dog—and it's got claws."

I took my time getting to the cave, thinking that the green monster was one of his scatterbrained notions.

"There," he said, pointing.

The lip of the cave was low and I had to stoop to see in. The water was clean and swirling. I saw claws and a pair of eyes, shining and black as night, sticking out at the end of two long stalks.

"It's a lobster," I said. "It's big. Leave it alone."

But Tom crawled into the cave. He fought the lobster for most of an hour, and I pulled them out, with the help of the stout girl, in a tangled mass of arms and claws. Tom caught three more lobsters in the cave, but none nearly so large as the monster, which was five feet long and a foot wide.

The camp feasted upon the day's gathering and smoked what was not eaten. Except for the palm hearts, we hadn't found any vegetables. But Admiral Somers had brought lettuce and onion seeds from England, which he planted, hoping they would grow.

Water was a problem after the first week. The casks we took from the wreck ran dry. There were no streams on the island where we were camped, but there were hundreds of small islands, a chain of them, to the east.

Governor Gates sent out a party in longboats to make a search for water. They found none, save pools where rain had collected. Then he had six shallow wells dug, found enough water for everyday use, laid out the ship's sails to catch run-off, and set up a small dam. The Reverend Bucke prayed for rain.

It came in a sudden burst that washed the dam away, downed the sails, and made us realize that we could not camp on the beach forever. Cedar, a fine, fragrant wood, grew on the island. Trees were cut and boards sawed, and carpenters put up a row of one-room huts roofed with palmetto. The construction went so well that Governor Gates announced he would soon set them to work building a ship that could take us all to Jamestown.

Through these few weeks I made no further attempts to free Anthony Foxcroft. But one night after supper, listening to Emma Swinton, I heard that some of the colonists were so taken with life in Bermuda they were laying secret plans to revolt against Governor Gates. They had no wish to leave this Eden when the ship he was planning to build sailed for Jamestown.

"One of the conspirators," she told me, "is Francis Pearepoint. He's one of the young gentlemen camped on the point out there by the *Sea Venture*."

"I know him. We talked on the ship once or twice."

"They call the camp Hampton Court," she said, "after the two-hundred-room palace of Henry the Eighth. They've found the wreck of an old Spanish galleon, I hear, and are searching around for gold. I hope they find it. I hope the conspiracy succeeds. I much prefer Bermuda to Jamestown, from what I know about it."

The moon was full. I walked down the beach to Hampton Court. The young gentlemen were sitting beside the fire, passing a long-stemmed pipe from one to the other. In front of them was a small chest with the lid thrown back. In it were some copper pots. Francis Pearepoint rose and bowed.

"You honor us with your presence, Miss Lynn. Please sit," he said, waving at a rock.

"Thank you," I said. "I'll stand."

"You come on a mission. A serious one, I see by your demeanor. May I be of help? I devoutly hope so."

"You can, sir. It's about Anthony Foxcroft."

"Yes, I know how brutally he's been treated. You and I talked about it once during the voyage. I again regret that I was not able to help in the matter. But things have changed. There's a ray of hope fluttering on the horizon."

"More than a ray," said one of the young gentlemen, Richard Knowles, I believe. "And more than fluttering. It's the sun itself coming up."

"We have an interesting thought," Francis Pearepoint said. "It comes from Hopkins, who, as you know, is well versed in the Scriptures. He believes, and we join him in believing, that it's no breach of honesty or religion to refuse to follow the rules Governor Gates has laid down. From the moment we were wrecked, the governor's authority ceased, Hopkins maintains. We are now free men, he says, absolutely free to conduct ourselves as we deem fit. Here we enjoy nature's richest bounties. To leave an earthly paradise for Jamestown, where people starve, die from the plague and arrows, is the sheerest folly."

"You and your friends and Stephen Hopkins may believe this, but you're only a part of the camp," I said.

"But an armed and determined part," Pearepoint said.

It was hopeful news, the best of news. A revolt against the governor, if it succeeded, would free Anthony Foxcroft.

Twelve

The next morning, as soon as it was light enough to make my way through the dense growth of palmetto trees, I set off to tell Anthony Foxcroft the news I had heard from Francis Pearepoint.

The moon, a ghost in a cloudless sky, shed no light. But I had taken the path each day since we came to the island and knew it well. The trees that huddled together, the quick shadows of dawn, the lingering shadows of dusk, the deep red sand that left no tracks, the many turnings—I knew them all.

Yet on this morning, as I hurried along, everything seemed different—the twisting path, the huddled trees, the far-off sound of waves on the beach. At last and for the very first time in all my visits, I carried wonderful news.

A fire burned in the clearing. A guard sat beside it, sleeping with one eye open. He had eaten something from a bowl, and a forest animal was nibbling at what he had left. The guard nodded when I spoke to him and uttered three words, words he always used as a greeting, whatever time of day it happened to be. "Good morning, miss," he said, and closed the eye that was open.

Anthony was in his hut, asleep. He had a hammock brought from the wreck, but he preferred sleeping on the sand and used the hammock for a pillow. Usually if I found him asleep, I returned to camp, leaving the gift I had brought—something special to eat from the settlers' table or a piece of clothing I had sewn, like a shirt made from a tattered sail. This morning I roused him with a kiss.

He raised his hands, shielding his eyes from the sun that suddenly bore down upon him through the trees. "You caused me an awful night," he said. "The lobster mixed with something that tasted like spoiled turnips gave me a vast ache in my belly." He stared up at me. "What did you bring today? Nothing to eat, I hope."

"I bring wonderful, cheering news."

He sat up and rested his manacled hands against his knees. "A ship has just arrived from England, bringing a pardon from the king? At this moment the ship waits off the coast to take me back to England? I'm to return in triumph, to the discomfort of Robert Carr, who is no longer the king's favorite?" He paused and wrinkled his brow. "Or Sir Thomas Gates has died from the turnip concoction that nearly caused my death last night?"

"You ate hearts of palm, not turnips, and they were delicious. Everyone said so, even Sir Thomas. I helped to make the dish myself."

He got up and began to pace. I let him pace. Finally he walked over and gave me a shake. "What?" he said. "What is the wonderful news?"

"Stephen Hopkins, the one who helps the Reverend Bucke at the meetings, who quotes the Scriptures," I began, and I told him the story that Francis Pearepoint had told me. "Pearepoint and his gentlemen are prepared to join Hopkins and depose the governor."

Anthony brightened. He had lost the awful ship's pallor.

The island sun had bronzed his skin. He had gained strength. He was as handsome as he had been before, even handsomer, because the brutal treatment suffered on the voyage had left a look in his eyes I had never seen before. As if he now viewed the world not as a heedless youth but as a man.

"Heartening news," he said, planting a kiss on my brow. "Bring me more when you come again."

"Tonight, perhaps, or tomorrow."

"I'll be here," he said, smiling, rattling his chains.

The camp was astir and breakfast fires were burning bright when I got back. The Reverend Bucke rang his bell. Stephen Hopkins called the roll. Two men were missing and their names were duly noted. The Reverend Bucke gave a short talk about how important it was for everyone to pitch in and repair the habitations, huts made of cedar boughs and thatched with palmetto leaves, that the storm had blown apart.

"God has given us a stint of halcyon nights and sunny days," he said, "but Satan squirms at God's gift. Expect him to send another rain and a spiteful wind upon us. Therefore work hard, this threat in mind, I pray you, and do not stop the day until everyone is properly sheltered."

Stephen Hopkins climbed onto the sandy mound that served as a pulpit. He prayed for a moment or two, then spoke about the limits of earthly power, freely quoting the Bible.

"Sir Thomas Gates," he said in a quiet voice. "Once in Jamestown he'll rule with a gentle hand, no doubt, according to the king's instructions. But here he feels all-powerful, the king himself, privileged to treat us as he chooses. We are not his slaves to be driven from one harsh task to another. Instead, we are free men, free to do as we see fit."

The Puritans and others of strong religious leanings, those who felt they had a covenant with God and the London Company, were silent as these words hung in the air. The rest of the camp muttered encouragement and urged him to go on.

"'Can two walk together,'" he said, quoting Amos, the herdsman, "'except they be agreed? Shall a trumpet be blown in the city and the people not be afraid?' Sir Thomas walks one way and many of us walk the other. The trumpet has sounded and I am letting it be known that we're afraid."

Before an hour had passed, Sir Thomas, who had not attended the morning sermon, heard the exact words Stephen Hopkins had spoken as he stood before the camp, repeated to him by a pair of Puritans, husband and wife. Hopkins was immediately summoned, and witnesses were called who testified against him. At nightfall he was sentenced to death.

Hopkins was treacherous, of course, guilty of outright rebellion, yet early the next morning two thirds of the camp hurried to his rescue. Led by Francis Pearepoint, Sir George Somers, and Captain Newport, they descended upon the governor, overpowered him with protests, and forced him to revoke the sentence. What's more, and it came quickly as I was about to call out Anthony's name, Francis Pearepoint raised his voice above the tumult.

"Foxcroft!" he shouted. "Foxcroft!"

His young gentlemen, who ranged behind him with their hands on the hilts of their swords, took up the name. Governor Gates stood with his back against a tree, squinting in the rising sun, covering his ears against the chant of "Foxcroft, Foxcroft."

Sir Thomas grew pale. His page put a hand out to steady him. The governor pushed it away and glanced about the crowd until he made out the stiff figure of the king's guard.

"Do you hold the key, Captain Fitzhugh?" he asked.

Fitzhugh hesitated and was silent. He was pushed forward by rough hands to where the governor stood against the tree.

"Give it over," the governor said.

Francis Pearepoint and his band rattled their swords and began to chant, "The key, the key, the key." Reluctantly, Fitzhugh reached in his jerkin and took out a key. But before he could hand it over, Pearepoint grabbed it and disappeared with his band.

I followed them along the path to the clearing and watched while they removed the manacles. I held my breath as they raised Anthony to their shoulders. I wept as they bore him off in triumph, like a hero.

The following day, having thought about what he had been forced to do and perhaps regretting it, the governor spoke to the camp. He seemed aware that the incident was clear warning of worse things to come.

"Our friends," he said, "are waiting to hear from us— those of our fleet who, I fervently pray, have arrived in Jamestown. Therefore I am sending a message to them that we are safe."

He called out our carpenters and set them to work on one of the longboats. Using hatches from the *Sea Venture*, they decked it over tightly, fashioned a short mast and a set of sails and oars, and provisioned it with food and water to last the many weeks that were necessary for the voyage to Virginia, hundreds of miles away.

The task was completed by the next morning. At breakfast Sir Thomas asked for six volunteers to man the longboat. Henry Ravens, mate of *Sea Venture*, came forward at once, as did Whittingham the purser, and two others.

A long silence followed. Wind had sprung up in the

night. The sky was heavily overcast and waves were pounding the wrecked ship. Almost every day had been fair since we landed on the island. We had forgotten about the hurricane. The lowering sky and crashing waves brought it to mind.

Governor Gates broke the silence. "It's a hazardous voyage to Jamestown," he said. "It's one I wouldn't choose to make myself, so I do not blame those who hesitate."

Samuel Sharpe jumped to his feet, moved by the words. His wife, who had a child in her lap, reached out and pulled him back.

"I'll not take men with wives or children, but thank you, Mr. Sharpe," the governor said, fixing his eye on Henry Shelly, a strapping young bachelor. Shelly raised his hand.

The governor said, "We now have five brave men. We need one more, but no one who is married."

His gaze moved over the silent ranks. I knew before it happened, before he stood up, a half-boyish, half-arrogant smile on his face, that Anthony would wait until all the men avoided each other's eyes and all were silent.

"Foxcroft," Anthony said, lifting his hand. "Anthony Foxcroft wishes to join the crew of the longboat bound for Jamestown and the New World."

A murmur ran through the crowd. Sir Thomas Gates caught his breath. It began to rain, and though he held his sugar-loaf hat against his chest, he didn't think to put it on.

Anthony said, "And I suggest, Governor Gates, since it's your concern for the rest of our fleet that prompts the voyage to Jamestown, the boat be christened *Gates' Gift,* in your honor."

The compliment brought a flush to the governor's cheeks. He stood with his sugar-loaf hat still clutched to his chest, the rain pouring down upon his head.

A voice came out of the crowd. "You don't dare to send

my prisoner to Jamestown," Captain John Fitzhugh shouted above the roar of the wind.

The governor roused himself. He put on his hat and said, "I dare to do what I wish. I wish to send Foxcroft to Jamestown. And since you are so attached to him, I send you also."

The crowd cheered. Fitzhugh shouted again, but a burst of wind whipped his words away. Captain Ravens called out, asking his men to gather, and Anthony hastened to join them.

The governor spoke to Henry Ravens. "As first mate on the *Sea Venture* you served me heroically," he said. "Now as captain of *Gates' Gift,* though she be little more than a cockleshell, you will again serve me heroically. Godspeed, and do not forget this when you are safe in Jamestown: Make every effort to find the princess Pocahontas and persuade her to grace the colony with her presence once more. Captain Newport has already spoken of her. I speak of this again because it is of the utmost importance.

"The first task, sir, I will set myself," Henry Ravens replied. "Though I fear it more difficult than getting our cockleshell across the western sea."

On his way through the cheering crowd, Anthony sought me out. Impulsively, my heart stopping, then starting up again, I grasped his hand to hold him back, as Samuel Sharpe's wife had held him back.

"You're crying," he said.

"It's not tears," I said. "It's rain."

"Let me see." He kissed my cheek. "The rain is salty," he said, and held my hand tight in his. "The sooner we reach Jamestown, the sooner this awful mess will end. And one day, much sooner that you think, we'll return to England, for the king has a short memory and a merciful heart. And Robert Carr, with his preening self-importance, may well be dead. We'll both be back at Foxcroft by the

River Dane at another masque, a more peaceful one, I am certain.''

He went on with his pretty speech while I clung to him. Then, suddenly he was gone, and his footsteps were lost in the sound of the rain and the wind threshing in the palmetto trees.

Thirteen

G*ates' Gift* slipped away before dawn two days later under the light of a moon in a cloudless sky. From the reef where the *Sea Venture* lay I watched the pinnace disappear.

That day Governor Gates began the building of a ship, which he named *Deliverance*. He called men together, including Francis Pearepoint's gentlemen, and explained how necessary it was for them, no matter how lacking their skills, to put a mighty effort into the building.

"We do not know if our fleet has arrived in Jamestown," he said, "and if it has, how many are fit for another voyage. We can't rely on Jamestown for any help at all. Without a ship we could be here for years, forever, stranded, helpless, forsaken."

Even more of the men wished to stay on the island than had in the beginning. The thought of starving in Jamestown or being scalped by Indians was less appealing than ever.

The governor now fully regretted the softness he had shown to Hopkins. He displayed his regret in the way he bit off his words and fixed a contemptuous eye upon Francis

Pearepoint, whom he regarded as the one most dedicated to his destruction.

He put Richard Frobisher, one of the ship's carpenters, in charge of the new ship.

Frobisher sent out a crew to dismantle the wreck and bring ashore every timber that could be used. He sent men into the woods to saw up the best cedars and shape them into planking. Others were set to work on the salvaged sails. After two days, the keel was laid and the *Deliverance* took shape, a bark half the size of the lost *Sea Venture*.

Then a lone sail was sighted far in the west. Admiral Somers, who was out exploring the numerous islands, reported that it belonged to the pinnace, that Captain Ravens had not been able to pass through the tangled chain of reefs.

On the third afternoon, he told us that Ravens had made his way at last through the maze of reefs and was headed off into the western sea.

Although it would take two weeks or more for the pinnace to reach Jamestown and as long for a rescue ship to return, the Puritans and the others who were impatient to leave built a beacon fire on a mount they called St. David's Hill. The beacon was lit every night as a symbol of devotion.

The building of *Deliverance* went fast for a few days. Then the work slowed down. Sir Thomas thought the men were bone-lazy. To set an example, when the bell rang for work he was at the ship in his old clothes, tools in hand, eager to undertake any task however menial.

His efforts failed. Those he thought shiftless were, in truth, a secret band of conspirators bent on delaying the work and destroying the ship if possible.

The day he learned of the conspiracy, he rounded up the ringleaders, six of them, who under duress admitted that they had planned to leave the camp and take one of the other islands for themselves. To grant their wish, the governor banished them to the farthest of the islands, all except the blacksmith and the shipwright, men whom he kept and put to work under threat of death.

It was a bad, disruptive time. The Reverend Bucke, whom everyone respected, got us together on the beach. It was a warm night, with a west wind, but black clouds and a tilted moon cast weird shadows on the gathering. A storm was in the offing. It seemed to suit our mood and the occasion.

After a short service, to which we responded in halting voices, the Reverend Bucke introduced Captain Newport, captain of the *Sea Venture*.

"We have reached the point," the captain said, "where neighbor quarrels with neighbor, where turmoil exists instead of peace. How, I ask, if this parlous state continues, can we ever reach Jamestown? And if by God's good grace we ever do, how can we be of help? I was there at Jamestown two years ago. First hand, I have seen its problems. They cannot be solved by this quarrelsome brood, be it one hundred fifty or one thousand fifty."

Lightning streaked the sky and rain poured down upon us. The Reverend Bucke shouted "Amen!" and we thoughtfully filed away.

Yet at this time, despite Newport's warnings, the governor and the admiral came to a falling out. They'd had small differences since the day we left Falmouth, more since the wreck. Now everything led to a lengthy argument and a parting.

Admiral Somers moved to the far end of the island and took with him twenty good workers, among them the square-jawed, square-wristed Tom Barlow, the young man I had talked to the night of St. Elmo's fire. Since I had taken notes and written letters for the admiral during the voyage, he asked me to join them.

The new camp was located on a pretty bay with a yellow cliff at one end and a stretch of white sand at the other end. Between them stretched a crescent of blue water so transparent that it seemed like air.

From my hut I looked across the bay to a small island covered with cedar trees not far from shore. To the east I could see the beacon fire they kept burning for Captain Ravens and his crew, for Anthony Foxcroft.

Admiral Somers had brought a boat with him, a small one taken from the wreck. He decided to make a chart of all the islands and the reefs, as well as a list of the trees, flowers, and wildlife he encountered. Tom Barlow would help with the boat, and I would come along with pen and paper to put down things he told me to, in the bold handwriting he admired.

Starting in the northeast on the point where *Sea Venture* was wrecked, we went west and south around the crescent, a great fishhook of land. Admiral Somers counted a chain of nearly a hundred islands and islets, took careful sightings, and had me write everything down. We didn't go ashore to explore any of the islands; that would come later, he said, when the chart was finished.

Two weeks after we had begun the chart, a bad storm hit the island and we couldn't go out. When the storm passed, we found the bay strewn with palm fronds, seaweed, reefs of dead birds, and shoals of fish.

"It was like the storm that wrecked *Sea Venture*," Tom Barlow said, "but not near so bad." He was thinking of Captain Ravens and Anthony Foxcroft. "Nothing to worry about much."

"I'm not worrying, Mr. Barlow."

"But you're quiet. And when you're quiet, you worry. Otherwise, you talk a lot."

Tom Barlow was rowing fast. We were trying to reach home before nightfall. Admiral Somers was looking at the chart, holding it up to catch the last of the sun. There was a bitter smell of smoke on the wind and the beacon fire flared up. Tom stopped rowing but kept his oar down. The boat turned back in a slow circle.

At first, when he dragged it out of the water, it looked like a patch of seaweed.

"Somebody's coat," he said, holding it up. "Likely belongs to one of the conspirators Sir Thomas banished. They're living over there on that island where the fire's burning."

I took the coat from him and knew as I touched it, as I saw on the breast, stitched in gold thread, the Foxcroft coat of arms, the crossed swords and lamb's head.

"Belongs to Anthony Foxcroft," Tom said. "He lost it overboard somehow. Easy to do in a longboat, everybody moving around, the boat bobbing . . ."

It was dark when we reached the shore. I took the coat and hung it away. It was possible that Anthony had lost the coat somehow, as Tom had said.

In the morning we went out again, but instead of rowing to the place where we had left off the day before, we went down the island toward the governor's camp. It made me suspicious.

The sun was hot and danced off the water. The beacon fire was dead. Wisps of pale smoke rose from the ashes. Men were standing around, and one of them held up a piece of wood, waved to us, and came down the beach to the water's edge.

The wood was splintered and no longer than the man's arm, but there were letters on it, carved deep and clear enough to read, the first six letters of the longboat's name.

"Foundered in the storm," Tom Barlow said.

The admiral shook his head. "Before that—the wood's bleached white."

A small flame leaped out from the dead beacon fire. This

smoke curled up from the ashes, then drifted away. Tom Barlow put the piece of wood down and took up the oars, and we went back along the island to where we had quit the night before.

Late in the morning of that day we found another piece of wreckage from Ravens' longboat. Near evening we found the boat's pointed stern.

The men no longer thought that Ravens and his crew could be alive. They had given up pretending that they were. They waited for me to say something. I glanced at the serpent ring and said nothing. I felt that at last the ring had failed me.

But later, as we silently went ashore, I remembered the king's words. He had said that the serpent ring would guard my life. My life, and no one else's life. Not even Anthony Foxcroft's life. But, and he had made this quite clear, the ring would not guard me from grief.

Fourteen

The building of *Deliverance*, the ship that was to carry us to Jamestown, had been dragging along despite the governor's best efforts. The day after the pieces of wood from the longboat were found, things quickly changed.

At dawn cannons went off at the far end of the island while we were eating breakfast. It was a summons from Sir Thomas Gates.

Drums were beating when we got to his camp. Everyone was gathered. Bugles called, and the Reverend Bucke prayed for a while. Then Sir Thomas strode out in his uniform, glittering with braid, and spoke for a short time.

I recall few of his words, except ones he kept repeating: "We owe a debt to these brave men."

Sir Thomas had a powerful voice, and his speech rang out through the camp, above the sound of the waves and the sad cries of the terns.

The governor asked us to work in the name of King James and the investors in London who had financed the voyage and to honor Captain Ravens and his brave crew who had given their lives to reach the desperate people in Jamestown. His impassioned call was heard and heeded.

None of the hewers of trees, none of those with menial tasks, remained absent. In the following two weeks alone, more was accomplished than during the two months just passed. But as the weeks passed and the bark neared completion, as the bare ribs were planked with cedar and the decks with oak salvaged from *Sea Venture*, workers became restless again.

Some wandered off and joined our camp, where *Patience*, the pinnace Admiral Somers had started, was growing but at a slower pace, for the admiral himself was in no hurry to leave Bermuda. Like him, they dreaded the time, fast approaching, when they would be forced by Sir Thomas to leave the land of blue skies, sparkling seas, and abundance.

Francis Pearepoint's gentlemen left the governor's camp, one by one, so as not to cause suspicion. They went off to the west, to the last island in the chain, where they had discovered the wreck of a second Spanish galleon.

When no treasure was found, they moved to our island and made camp, not to work but no conspire. Since the conspirators outnumbered the loyalists, they came to believe that it would be possible to seize the cannons, the guns, the supplies and—at last—to murder Sir Thomas Gates. In the words of Admiral Somers, " 'twas a devilish time."

If he himself was not a conspirator, the admiral still favored the cause. Pearepoint became the leader but carefully kept in the background while pushing one of his followers, Henry Paine, to the fore. The only one in our camp who stood up for the governor was Tom Barlow. But the only influence he had was on me, and I had none at all.

"Where do you stand?" he asked when the conspiracy had reached its height and Pearepoint was ready to move against the governor. "You seem not to care what happens."

"I don't."

"You're awfully anxious to get back to England."

"I am."

"Listen, Miss Lynn, remember that you put your name on a contract with the Adventurers of London. They paid your passage money to Jamestown. You owe them work and dutiful obedience."

"They took a chance, they gambled on me, and I nearly lost my life. The rest of my life, what is left of it, is mine. I owe the Adventurers nothing more."

"A lightsome way to look at a solemn promise, I must say, a contract made in good faith and duly signed."

"You talk like John Calvin, the preacher," I said angrily. "You look like him, too. You're a Calvinist, no doubt."

It was the night before the happening, and the conspirators, more than twenty of them, had eaten and gone off to hold one of their secret talks, not trusting us.

In the firelight Tom Barlow did have a Calvinistic look, at least as I pictured Calvin from my brief readings—tall, thin, a high forehead, and, almost hidden beneath heavy brows, black eyes, not cold but darkly penetrating.

He liked dried turtle meat and had a piece of it in his mouth which he was talking around. "What's more," he said, "the colony at Jamestown is named for the king. Before we left Plymouth, His Majesty sent his blessings to our fleet by messenger, wishing it Godspeed. Is your desire to return to England the proper answer? Besides a contract with the Adventurers, you have one that's far more binding, a contract with His Majesty, King James of England."

The king's name, spoken in Tom Barlow's deep voice, hung accusingly on the night wind.

"What, what will you do?" Tom Barlow said. "Where do you stand? For Governor Gates or for Admiral Somers?"

"For the king!" I said. "Of course, for King James."

"Then you stand with Gates against Somers and the conspirators."

"If he is a conspirator, why is he building a boat to help us reach Jamestown? It's nearly finished."

"A ruse. You'll see an uprising soon."

"Does Governor Gates know he's in danger?"

"He's looking for trouble at any time. Ordered his men to wear weapons during the day and to sleep with them at night. Only a few loyalists are left, but they're better armed than the conspirators."

"You're one of the few loyalists," I said. "What are you going to do if there's trouble?"

"You'll see."

His eyes glistened in the firelight. I had a strong feeling that much of what Governor Gates knew about our camp, its secret meetings, the plan to gather arms, the talk about setting up a new colony on Bermuda with Admiral Somers as its governor, he had learned straight from Tom Barlow.

"You'll get yourself killed," I said.

His eyes still glistened. He thrust out a subborn chin. "Perhaps. Yet a man has to be loyal to his given word. If he isn't, he might as well be dead."

In the firelight I could see the face of John Calvin, gangling Calvin, the preacher.

The following afternoon we heard cannon fire, the signal for everyone to gather at the governor's camp. The admiral, Tom Barlow, and I were in the bay, working along a reef, fishing for supper. We had caught a boatload of bass and gray snapper to smoke. Also four tunny that must have weighed six hundred pounds between them.

Admiral Somers kept on fishing when the cannon went off. But Tom Barlow pulled in his line, took up the oars, and began to row toward the governor's camp. The admiral kept his line in the water and acted as if the only thing on his mind was fishing. I knew better.

Close to dusk, after a hard row, two boats from our camp edged up to shore some distance from the governor's camp. The weapons Pearepoint had managed to bring were hidden under a blanket of palmetto leaves, and the boats were put in the charge of one of his men.

Governor Gates was waiting for us in front of the stocks he had ordered on the day we came to the island. In the stocks, his hands and his bushy head thrust out through the holes, languished Henry Paine. Paine, one of the stalwart young gentlemen, was the governor's trusted guard. But unknown to the governor he was in league with Francis Pearepoint. Apparently he had been in the stocks the previous night and kept awake since, for his eyes were red and half-closed.

The governor gave our party a searching glance to make sure, no doubt, that none of our men was armed. He then turned to Henry Paine.

"Is it true," he shouted, "that last night when called upon to take your watch, you hurled insults upon the captain of the guards, struck him on the head with your fist, and took yourself off, scoffing at the double watch I had ordered?"

Henry Paine opened his eyes but did not answer.

"Furthermore, when told that if word of your behavior ever reached my ears it might mean your life, you brazenly replied, 'The governor has no authority to justify upon anyone an action of that nature. Therefore, let the governor kiss . . .' 'kiss my . . .' 'my foot.' Or some such insulting remark."

Henry Paine was obviously surprised at the governor's violent tone. "I don't recall such words. I never intended. . . . There must be a mistake."

"The mistake is yours, Mr. Paine. And for it you shall pay."

"But, sir, I have paid enough already," Paine said.

He glanced at Pearepoint. I was sure that the two had made a pact, that Paine had deliberately provoked a fight with the governor, and at this moment, armed with an excuse and according to plan, Pearepoint and his men were to attack Sir Thomas and set up their own government.

Pearepoint coldly returned his glance. He did not move. Why I am not sure. Was it because the governor, suspecting a plot, had placed two of his cannons and four of his cannoneers on either side of the stocks, and stood with a solid wall of cedar trees at his back? Surprised by this, had Pearepoint decided to put off his attack until a more favorable time? It seemed likely.

"You shall pay dearly," the governor said. "You shall pay with your life."

A cry went up from Mistress Horton and others, for Henry Paine was well liked in the camp. But the governor called for a ladder, which was set up under a tree.

Paine tried to squirm out of the holes that held him. Failing this, he leveled his gaze upon Pearepoint, saw no hope there, and began to talk to the governor, admitting his guilt and asking for mercy.

The governor turned his back. He ordered a noose and saw that it was attended properly, with a double bend and a sailor's knot, to a stout branch.

Paine studied the noose, which was moving about in the evening wind, frowned, and said, "Since I am a gentleman, I own the privileges thereof and demand that I be shot instead of hanged like a commoner."

"Your demand is granted," the governor said. "And may God forgive you, as I willingly do."

The sun went down as these words were spoken. Our group left and climbed into the boats. We had not gone far when I heard two shots. Wisps of smoke drifted up through the palmetto trees.

Pearepoint shook a fist at the camp, at the settlers who

were now cheering the governor. "We'll return and soon," he said.

Admiral Somers was silent. He put out his fishing line and told Tom Barlow to row toward a reef where a school of yellowtails roiled the water. Tom bent his back and rowed hard. He kept glancing at me, trying to make out how I felt about the governor and what he had done.

Finally he said, "The governor has taken a lot from Paine and the rest. I don't blame him, do you?"

"I question what will happen at Jamestown. Will he shoot everyone who acts up or disagrees? Now that he's shot one, it may get to be a habit."

"We'll put a halter on him with obedience and love."

"You may do so, but not I."

"You'll change your mind once you gaze upon the wonders of the New World."

"No," I said. "It's idle to think so."

Tom set his jaw and rowed even harder toward the school of leaping fish.

Fifteen

No one in either of the two camps had expected Sir Thomas Gates to act so suddenly and with such cold fury. He had mildly punished other traitors by sending them off to another island. He had intended to hang Stephen Hopkins but had been persuaded not to.

The death of Henry Paine, therefore, came as a shock to everyone, to those who, though loyal to the governor, had accused him of being soft-hearted. And a lesson to Francis Pearepoint and his gentlemen, who had grandly thought to depose him.

It encouraged the loyalists to take a stand behind Sir Thomas. It cautioned the dissenters to mend their ways lest they, too, should join the late Henry Paine. And it spread calm upon troubled waters.

Hitherto Admiral Somers held prayers on Sunday morning, himself preaching a short sermon and Tom Barlow rendering a song or two in his resounding voice. Now we rowed to the main camp and listened to the Reverend Bucke while Sir Thomas stood by with a sharp eye, smiling kindly.

Months passed, and the coming of spring coincided with some happy events. Elizabeth Persons, maid to Mistress

Horton, was married to Thomas Powell, Sir George's cook. Elizabeth was tall and plain and Thomas was tall and handsome, which was not a good combination, as time would prove. I lent Elizabeth my pretty palmetto fan, adorned with pearls that Tom Barlow had gathered on the shore and given me. The wedding took place beneath a bower of pink roses, with wild bursts of musketry.

Then Mistress and John Rolfe's daughter was baptized and given a name. Mistress Horton, who, next to Emma Swinton, had the prevailing voice among our women, suggested three names for the baby—Mary, Celeste, and Ruth. But none of these was chosen. Governor Gates liked the name Bermuda, so this was the name she was called.

Sir George and Sir Thomas met often and discussed the barks they were building separately. After a spring storm tossed *Deliverance* about on her beam-ends and the governor decided to put up a bulkhead to protect her, the admiral sent men into the hills to bring rocks and timber.

When *Deliverance*, the big ship built to carry most of the people, and *Patience*, the small pinnace built for the rest, were launched, both camps turned out and happily feasted upon palmetto hearts, mussels, clams and lobster, turtle stew and roast pig. Tom Barlow played his viola and sang.

During the following two weeks everyone helped to gather food. Terns were not so plentiful as they had been the day we came to the island, but we managed to fill a barrel with their eggs. Turtles were coming ashore, scooping out deep holes and laying their eggs—as many as five hundred at a time—and covering them with sand for the sun to hatch. Of these, over six thousand were gathered and set down in brine. Fish of all kinds still swarmed the blue waters. Admiral Somers, Tom Barlow, and I caught more than a ton one afternoon, which were smoked and stored away for the voyage.

Deliverance and *Patience* rode at anchor five days, waiting for a westerly wind to take them through the narrow

channel into the sea. On the tenth of May the wind shifted
from the east. Admiral Somers and Captain Newport went
off to buoy the way, the only way we could sail.

Governor Gates set up in the admiral's garden a *mnemos-
ynon*, a fair memorial of our experience on the island of
Bermuda. It was made from the timber of our ruined ship in
the figure of a cross and was fastened to a mighty cedar. In
the center of the cross the governor placed a silver
twelvepence, which bore the picture of King James.

The Reverend ﹏﹏﹏ spoke a short prayer, drums beat,
horns blew, from ﹏﹏ *eliverance* came two loud cannon
shots. But ﹏﹏﹏﹏ one was glad to be sailing off to
Jamestown. I dare say that if a vote had been taken, more
than half of the settlers would have voted to remain among
the palmetto trees and the blue waters.

By ten o'clock the next morning everyone was aboard.
Tom Barlow and I were on the *Patience* with Admiral
Somers and all of the gentlemen. The rest were aboard
Deliverance.

The wind was light now, and the big ship had to be towed
with a longboat. Even then, the channel was so narrow and
twisting that she struck on the starboard side, fortunately
not hard enough to split her planking. With shallow water
on one side and jagged rocks on the other, we followed in
her wake under a single sail into the open sea.

The wind served us well that day, so easily that, unlike
my departure from Plymouth, I never felt a seasick
moment. It held fair, though sometimes scarce and often
contrary, during which we twice lost sight of the
Deliverance.

Shortly after dawn on the seventeenth of May, Admiral
Somers spied a change in the sea and said we were not far
from land. Dead trees and rubbish floated past from time to
time.

That night he took soundings with the dipsey lead and
found that we were sailing in thirty-seven fathoms of water.

On the twentieth, near midnight, a marvelously sweet smell, sweet beyond belief, engulfed us.

Next daybreak a sailor in the foretop of *Deliverance* descried land. We had no cannon on *Patience*, but Tom Barlow fired his musket, and we all cheered, even Pearepoint and his men, who no doubt felt that the sooner they reached Jamestown the sooner they could return to Bermuda and their search for gold.

The following day we entered a broad expanse of water. Admiral Somers called it the Chesapeake and said, "It's a fairer bay than any I have ever seen."

Later we came upon a bluff some two miles distant, where a fort that sat at the entrance to the James River was located. Its captain discharged a warning shot at us, thinking we might be Spaniards. Governor Gates went off in a longboat to assure him we were friends and English. When he returned, he signaled to Admiral Somers and we moved up to where *Deliverance* lay anchored.

Sir Thomas was standing at the rail, dressed in light armor, hand on the hilt of his sword. He looked grim and didn't speak until aroused.

"What did you find?" Somers asked him. "Did our fleet reach Jamestown safely?"

"Safe all six, save the pinnace *Catch*, which was set adrift."

"What of Captain Ravens and the longboat?"

"Not seen, not seen, of course," Sir Thomas said. "Lost, as well we know, long ago on that day the debris washed in." He gave me a gentle look. "It is good to know the truth, is it not? And not to live your life and die a little each day."

I did not answer. In the cloudy sky high above us, gray birds were screaming. I let their wild, sad cries answer for me.

BOOK THREE

Jamestown, Virginia

Sixteen

Tides and shifting winds held us for a day. Then a gentle breeze carried us up the James to a point of land and Jamestown. Below the settlement, tall trees overhung the riverbank. Sailors tied the two ships to the trees, quietly, as if they were tying a pair of horses. Sir Thomas Gates shouted for everyone to line up in orderly fashion and not to move until he gave the order.

Deliverance fired her cannon. Muskets roared. Bugles sounded. Everyone cheered. Sir Thomas shouted for quiet.

Signaling us to follow, he strode ashore and took a path that led upward to a huddled settlement atop a hillock. He held his sword aloft. His scarlet cloak fluttered in the wind and showed a glint of gold braid. Beside him, right and left, drummers beat upon their drums. We followed, singing a sprightly tune. It was a fine display, meant to hearten all the citizens of Jamestown.

But tramping along behind Sir Thomas, I thought it curious that the path we followed was overgrown with weeds and doubly curious that no one from the settlement had come to greet us.

Above me, at the end of the weed-grown path, I caught a

glimpse of a stockade with most of the stakes missing, the sagging roof of what was once a fort, a row of ruined huts. Had the settlers left? Had Jamestown been abandoned? If so, Sir Thomas surely would have been told when he talked to those at Fort Comfort.

He came to a halt in front of the stockade. Through the gate, which hung loose on its hinges, stumbled a grizzled old woman, leading a child. Behind her stood a cluster of silent figures. The woman wanted to know if the ships had brought food.

Sir Thomas, though shocked by the desolation that lay around him, by the starving woman and the silent figures, said in a hearty voice, "Two shiploads, good lady. Fish, eggs, turtle meat, strings of smoked birds. We'll spread a grand feast for you ere the sun goes down."

"Now would be the better," the old woman said. "A little now. Some of us will not be here when the sun goes down."

"So now it is," Sir Thomas said in the same hearty voice, and sent a bevy of guards headlong to the ships.

The child wandered over and grasped the hem of my skirt. She had blue eyes and corn-colored hair that needed combing.

"What name do you have?" I asked her.

"Humility," she said. "And my mother's name is Humility, too."

"It's a pretty name. How nice. Where is your mother?"

"In heaven," the child said. "My father is in heaven, too. I will see them soon."

Our people crowded around the ruined gate and stared at those inside. Emma Swinton, holding the red parasol saved from the wreck, came up with a quiet tread to where I stood.

"It's not safe for the child to pull at your skirt," Swinton said. "She has dirty hands and soiled feet. She may have the plague, for all we know."

At these words, Humility backed away. I picked her up. She was all bones, light as a starving sparrow.

Emma Swinton snapped the parasol shut and made a sign with it.

I had seen the sign before. The first time on the day we left Plymouth. Once again on the day before we were struck by the violent storm. It was made then with a finger. Now it was made with the red parasol, as her eyes rested gently upon the child.

Our people gazed at the ruined fort and the tumbled barricade and the starving. They must have wished, all of them except our leaders and the Reverend Bucke, that they were back in the soft airs of Bermuda, among the palm trees and the blue water and bounteous shoals of food, just for the taking. Their groans were tight-lipped and silent, but I heard them nonetheless.

Barrels of smoked pork were trundled up the hill. Governor Gates had them opened for all to see, but the starving people hung back.

"Step up, my friends," he said in his stentorian voice. "There are more barrels of pork, barrels of fish, and birds laid down in fat awaiting you."

The starving people just stared at the tempting food, too weak to move.

A man standing beside the governor said, "It's been a terrible time. We've had scarce a handful of corn each day. This, for weeks now. The smell of food, the mere sight of it, must make them ill as it does me. Bear with us, I pray you. We'll soon get our stomachs back."

The man, I learned, was Sir George Percy. He had been president of the colony since the day Captain Smith was badly burned in a fire and forced to return to England.

The colony had fared well under Smith's guidance. This I remembered from what was said about him at the countess of Foxcroft's masque. He had frowned on laziness. Those who did not work did not eat. Those who disobeyed orders were punished. He went boldly among the Indians, often alone, threatening them if himself threatened, carrying out his threats if need be.

But no more than sixty of the some five hundred settlers had survived the past six months. "A deathly winter," Sir George Percy said as he stood gazing at the food spread out upon the grass, still unable to touch it.

"We called it 'the Starving Time.' We ventured outside the fort only to bury our dead, but only at night in shallow graves, for the earth was frozen and we feared death from savage arrows. Inside the fort stalked famine and pestilence. Huts of the dead and pickets from the stockade were burned for firewood. So great was the famine that an Indian we managed to slay was consumed. One amongst our starving slew his wife and was secretly eating her when discovered. Truly, a Starving Time. My friends, if you had not come at this fateful hour, we all would have been dead within the week."

Percy grasped the hilt of his sword to salute Governor Gates but lacked the strength to take it from the scabbard.

Little of the food we brought was eaten that day, and those who did eat it fell ill.

Three died in the night; one of them was the grizzled old woman who had befriended the child. I held Humility close while the grave was dug. Afterward I gathered her clothes— a pair of red striped hose that needed mending—and got permission from Captain Newport to take her aboard the *Deliverance*.

As I glanced at the ruined fort, the roofless church, the tumbled barricade, I stopped as though smitten by a club. My dearest wish was to return to England, to the position with Queen Anne that the king had promised me.

I had learned in my brief time at Jamestown more of what I had learned from Captain John Smith at Foxcroft. Princess Pocahontas had not only saved his life, but she also had saved the first colonists. But when, desperately ill, he had gone back to England without saying good-bye to her, she had not set foot in Jamestown again.

Chief Powhatan, her father, was the ruler of a vast part of Virginia and twenty-eight different tribes. An emperor, a despot, he ruled the confederacy with a spear and a war club. When his daughter stopped her visits to Jamestown and the governors of the colony treated him arrogantly, he had sworn to sink every English ship on the James River and leave the settlement in ashes.

He adored his daughter and was said to indulge her slightest whim. Since the colony had survived during the time she had visited it and brought food, and since she was responsible for his grudging good will, it was clear to me that the princess must be found and persuaded to make friends with the colony once again. And I must undertake it.

It was a wild idea. It would help Jamestown. Selfishly, somehow it would help me get back to England. I went with the idea to Admiral Somers, who looked upon the scheme with a dubious eye. But Governor Gates, who didn't much care whether I lived or perished, and William Strachey, who thought the same, believed it might succeed.

The next day I was sent off with a flourish of trumpets, ten stout soldiers, and an old Indian, Mary Soltax, to serve as an interpreter. It was thought that Pocahontas would most likely be found far up the Pamunkey River in a village called Werowocómoco, where the most important temple in all of her father's vast domain was located.

"If the princess is not there," Governor Gates said as I settled myself on the barge, "they will know where she is." He raised his sword in salute. "Fare thee well," he shouted.

"We await your safe return. We will remember you in our daily prayers."

Prayers? I did not seek his prayers. Safe? It had never crossed my mind that I would not be safe. The serpent ring, its thrice-wound coils, its jeweled, half-closed eyes that never shut, was tight upon my finger.

Seventeen

The third day of our voyage by oar and sail, following a map Captain Smith had made years before, we came to the Pamunkey River. From here after a day's travel, still following the captain's map, we sighted a village that we took to be Werowocómoco.

Before we could land, a fleet of canoes filled with painted warriors came out to meet us. They surrounded the barge, screeched in high-pitched voices, and brandished clubs. But when they saw that two of our party were women, their deportment changed. Smiling, chattering like magpies, they escorted us onward. Since our barge grounded before we had gone far, two of the warriors carried Mary Soltax and me ashore.

Speaking in the Algonquian dialect, Mary told their leader, a muscular young man shining with bear grease, why we had come. Of what she said, I understood only two words: Powhatan and Pocahontas.

Forthwith, we were led through a stretch of sandy ooze and up a hillside to the village—a crooked street of huts and, at the end of the street, a long house. Our soldiers refused to give up their weapons but were made to lie down among a stand of trees, while we were shown to a place where fires burned and women were cooking. No men were in sight, albeit dozens of boys silently watched us from various outposts.

We sat for a time unattended, then three tall fellows painted half-black, half-red, with white eyes and red strokes on their cheeks, came and danced. They wore robes made of blackish snakes stuffed with moss, the tails tied together in tassels.

They danced for a long time, shouting invocations in hellish voices. I had the impression that we were being purified, made fit to converse with the great werowance, Chief Powhatan.

Presently we were led into a templelike hut, fashioned of tree boles and woven reeds, and seated upon mats. We were brought water to wash our hands and turkey-feather towels to wipe them.

Afterward we were served bowls of thick gruel. I ate mine and found it wholesome, but Mary Soltax, thinking no doubt that the mush might be poisoned, only made a show of eating.

From the far end of the temple came the sound of rattles. To their accompaniment a large figure, undoubtedly Chief Powhatan, surrounded by a phalanx of half-naked warriors, made his way to a throne covered with hides. A girl who had followed him arranged herself at his feet.

By the light of a fire blazing in front of the throne, I saw that the emperor was an elderly man with a small, gray beard and a grim countenance. He wore a mantle of raccoon skins, their ringed tails cascading down his front. His neck was looped with chains of gleaming pearls.

The girl's face was turned away from me, yet I felt, from the tilt of her head, the chain of jeweled seashells around her neck, that she was the princess Pocahontas.

I had come only to speak to her, but realizing that first I

must address her father, I got to my feet and pulled Mary, the interpreter, up beside me, instructing her to say that I was immensely honored to be in the presence of Chief Powhatan, werowance of all the waters.

Mary took her time and stretched out my few words into a lengthy greeting of some sort. To which the chief replied with a wave of his hand and silence.

His gaze was fixed upon a statue standing near me. The Reverend Bucke had one like it, which he once used in a sermon to warn the settlers of what barbarians they had to deal with. It was a statue of Okeus, the most powerful of the Powhatan gods, a wooden crosspiece as tall as a man, padded out with moss, hung with pearls, the body painted black and the mossy face the color of white flesh.

The chieftain said a few words which Mary Soltax did not catch but which caused howls of laughter from the phalanx of warriors ranged at his back. His heavy gaze shifted from the effigy to a large rough stone that stood between him and the fire. Was this the altar that Captain Smith had told me about, upon which his head had been held while a warrior crouched above him with a knotted club?

I trembled, but not from fear of my life, only from the fear that Powhatan would never allow his daughter to speak. He was in a sullen mood. Was he thinking back to the time when she had defied him and thrown herself upon the outstretched body of John Smith? Possibly I should address him and not Pocahontas.

She had been listening to his every word. Now she had turned and was studying me through a curtain of black hair that nearly hid her face.

"White girl," she said suddenly and to my great surprise, speaking English words haltingly but in a clear, low-pitched voice. "You have come to take me away. You wish that I will come to Jamestown now, tomorrow, if not tomorrow, soon."

She tossed back the black curtain of hair. Her eyes, which were set deep and far apart, aslant at the corners, blazed.

"You will ask me this," she said, "because you are starving over there in that place. And I will not go there because you do not wish me, Pocahontas. All you wish is a large canoe heaped with corn so you can eat and not die."

The emperor broke in to grumble a few words and a string of names, which Soltax interpreted. "He says that the white men want corn. Corn and also the land he rules from Werowocómoco to the Chickahominy, to Nansemonds, to the cypress groves of Uttamussack. All of it the white man wants and which the white man shall not have."

The emperor's eyes shifted back and forth between the altar and the statue of Okeus, the god of evil who brought sickness, ruined the ripening corn, stirred up wars, and ravaged the land with storms. A god who must be constantly appeased lest he destroy the world itself. It was from the god's savage demands that John Smith had been saved.

Pocahontas was still looking at me, her head half-turned, but in her gaze I saw a faraway look, as if she were thinking of a different time.

"Before I came to your country," I said, "I talked to Captain Smith."

The faraway look disappeared, albeit there was no other sign that the name meant anything to her.

"You will remember him?"

She nodded.

"He spoke affectionately of you. He called you his beautiful little princess."

"I was a child then."

In the firelight, her skin had had the brightness of burnished copper. I saw it change and take on a deeper hue.

"The captain told me how you had saved his life."

Her eyes changed. They glowed. They glistened like living coals.

"And more, you had saved the lives of many in Jamestown who were starving. I came to ask you to come to Jamestown again as you used to do. Then your father will look upon us more kindly. Then we will have more food to eat. Then we will not live every day fearful of being attacked. And you will not be fearful of us."

As I said these words I was aware that her father was right, that the colonists meant to take over his land. It would disappear, piece by piece, stream by stream, river by river, from the sea to the mountains and beyond. Still, I had come here to help Jamestown and in so doing to help especially my chances of returning to England.

Chief Powhatan listened, though he understood nothing of what we had said. He scratched his scanty beard and was silent, more sullen than ever. He had never once looked at me and didn't now. His gaze was set fast upon his daughter.

I felt uncomfortable. I am certain she also felt uncomfortable under his sullen gaze. I had said all that I could say to her. I hoped that my words had kindled a forgotten memory. But feeling that if I stayed for another moment something awful would happen, I rose with dignity and bowed to the emperor, who averted his eyes.

Pocahontas jumped to her feet. The emperor restrained her with a heavy hand, with what must have been an Indian oath. She flung his hand aside and embraced me. Presently men in yellow robes appeared from out of the bitter smoke and violently tore us apart.

In fear of our lives, Soltax and I hurried from the scene, past the sacrificial fire and the piled stones of the altar. At the temple door I stopped and looked back. Pocahontas was being led away. Would we ever, ever meet again?

Eighteen

I was no sooner back at the fort, having failed to bring Pocahontas with me, than the High Council—Governor Gates, Admiral Somers, Secretary Strachey, and others—met together in a short session. Without a dissenting voice, they voted to abandon the colony and return to England.

Four days after their decision, to a stir of drums and a fusillade of musketry, we left Jamestown and moved down the river on our way to the sea. We were not out of sight when the Indians swarmed into the deserted fort. Their flaming brands glowed in the dusk.

We anchored at the mouth of the river and ate supper on the deck of *Deliverance*. It was a happy feast, for most everyone was glad to be going home to England—not only the survivors of the awful winter, but also the newcomers shocked by the desolation they had seen.

As for me, I was the happiest person at the feast.

Already I was across the endless sea. I was home in Foxcroft, at my desk in the tower, about to write a letter to James, King of England, Scotland, and Ireland. But what could I say? I cudgeled my brain. I got up from the desk. I peered out the window at the River Dane flowing sweetly in the meadow.

The king wouldn't know that I had followed Anthony Foxcroft to Plymouth and beyond. He'd think that I had been seized by the New World fever, a fever that he himself had kindled. But would he look kindly upon the fact that I had turned down his kingly offer to be a secretary to his wife, Queen Anne? Would he? If not, what then?

The feast lasted well into the night. Survivors had regained their taste for food and consumed great quantities of it, to the point that before the feast was over, Somers grew alarmed that our supplies wouldn't last till we reached England.

Even six-year-old Humility, comforted by the thought that both her father and mother were in heaven and she would see them soon, ate like a grown-up, some of everything, but two of the big turtle eggs, which she had never tasted before. I told her how the turtles swam out of the sea, dug holes in the sand, laid their eggs, and covered them up, and how later on, often on a moonlit night, the eggs hatched and the tiny turtles crawled down to the sea and swam away.

Humility got up and quietly disappeared.

"She's a pretty child," Emma Swinton said. "But she's in dire need of guidance. Prettiness can lead to sin, you know. She needs a Christian mother."

"You'll have to ask Governor Gates about that," Tom Barlow said.

"I'll do so tonight. There's no time to lose. The devil never nods."

I left the two of them arguing about the devil. I found Admiral Somers, who again was in charge of the expedition now that we were going to sea, and told him that I liked Humility and wanted to take care of her.

"Legally?" he asked.

"Legally, beginning now, if you please."

"There are papers to sign. We'll attend to them in the morning."

"Why papers? Why can't I just take her?"

"Steal her, like a gypsy? No, it's the law."

"Then remember that I asked for her first. Someone else wants her."

"Who?"

"Emma Swinton."

"I'll remember," the admiral said. "I'll remember well."

But the papers were not signed the next day. An hour after sunrise, as the tide turned and Admiral Somers made ready to depart with the current, a lookout on *Deliverance* called down from his lofty mainmast perch. Everyone crowded to the rail.

"Sails!" the lookout shouted.

A gray mist swirling low along the river made phantom shapes that looked like castles.

"It can't be," Governor Gates shouted back.

"Sails," the lookout shouted. "A fleet. Sailing slow against the current."

"No ship sails against the current," the governor told him angrily, "slow or otherwise. Look again!"

There was a short silence. Then the lookout said, "Five ships, sir. Coming slow against the current on the starboard tack, sir. Could be Spaniards."

Governor Gates stiffened at the word "Spaniards." Enemies of England, they were strongly placed in habitations along the southern coast and on the islands of the Caribbean Sea, ready to pounce upon the rich lands of Virginia now that Jamestown lay abandoned.

He took a step toward the mainmast, as if to climb to the tower where the lookout crouched. Instead, he shouted,

"Do you see markings, Spanish markings? The cross and the castle of Castile?"

"Nothing of the kind, sir. And the ships are rigged the English way. It's an English fleet, five ships heading straight toward us. And against the current, sir."

"If they sail against the current, they're English."

Admiral Somers, dismayed by the conversation, spoke up. "Come, come, there's no fleet, English, Spanish, or otherwise, that sails against this current. More than likely the fleet's not sailing at all. It's anchored and we are sailing toward it."

This proved to be true. In less than an hour we overtook the five ships.

They were anchored at Mulberry Isle, waiting for the tide to turn. All were larger than ours and they were not Spanish. The flag of St. George flew at the mainmasts and, around the largest ship, just below the railings, ran a waistcloth emblazoned with an English coat of arms.

"I recognize the ship and its waistcloth. She belongs to Lord De La Warr," Admiral Somers said.

"To think that if we had sailed an hour sooner," Governor Gates said, "whilst the river was still fogged, we would have missed him."

The Reverend Bucke fell to his knees. Cannons roared aboard the *Deliverance* and a ragged round of musketfire sounded from the *Patience*. Settlers crowded to the rails. A few cheered, but most were confused or outright stunned.

To me, it was a bitter disappointment—De La Warr's five ships anchored there in the river, flags waving, decks crowded with settlers. Our people, despite what they had lived through, waved back. It meant that my dreams of England had come to an end.

Tom Barlow, beside himself with joy, couldn't speak. He lifted Humility to the rail so she could see the ships.

"What are they?" she asked.

"New settlers," I said, "in five big ships."

"Where are they going?"

"To Jamestown."

"It is a bad place. Why are they going to Jamestown? There's nothing in Jamestown anymore."

"To start a new colony."

"Why?"

"Because" was the best answer I could give her.

"Where are *we* going?"

"Back to Jamestown."

She gave me a fearful look.

"Jamestown's saved by a miracle," a shrill voice said.

It was Emma Swinton, elbowing her way toward us, reaching out for Humility.

"You are saved, too, dear child," she said, "snatched from the sinful life of English sinners. I know Foxcroft. It's a sinful place."

As she reached for Humility, picking at her with bony fingers, I clasped the child.

"She's mine, she's mine," Emma Swinton kept saying.

I turned my back. With a threat, she hustled off, calling out for Admiral Somers.

Tom Barlow said to comfort the child, "The ships are stuffed with food. Now you'll have lots to eat. All you can eat every day and in the middle of the night."

I didn't think the child heard him. She was trembling, staring at the ships.

Tom looked at me, his eyes on fire. I imagined he was shaggy John Calvin, as I always did.

"Like this child, you are also saved from sin," he said.

I walked away, still clutching Humility, and found a place on the sterncastle deck where the fleet was hidden from view. The wide river stretched far out to sea.

"There'll be a ship sailing back to England one of these days," I said to Humility, "and we'll sail with her. We'll sail to where I live. I live in a tower and you'll live with me. And you'll have lots to eat every day."

Humility smiled. "Promise?" she asked.

I crossed my heart and promised, but I doubted this day would ever come.

Tom Barlow appeared and said, "Somers is in command until we're on shore and De La Warr takes over. I'll talk to him about the child."

He came back before we landed at Jamestown with a scribbled paper signed by Admiral Somers. It did not give me the right to claim Humility as my daughter but did give me the right, so long as we were in Virginia, to serve as her guardian. The gift brightened the hour.

Nineteen

We sailed with the tide and led Lord De La Warr's fleet up the James.

Silence gripped our ship when the abandoned fort loomed through the mist. It was strange to return to the ghostly place we had departed just the day before, never to return. I do believe that Tom Barlow was the only happy one among us.

Attired in slashed red velvet, Lord De La Warr leaped ashore and beckoned us up the hillock where the church had stood. Here, flanked by fifty liveried attendants, his standard-bearer read the terms of De La Warr's commission. The Reverend Bucke held a short thanksgiving service, and then the noble lord spoke at length in a voice that would have shaken the rafters had there been any to shake.

"We shall rebuild the church," he said. "We shall rebuild the fort and build new forts down the river, two of them, to be called Fort Henry and Fort Charles in honor of the two sons of our king. We shall restore and strengthen the palisades and bulwarks. The church will be larger than before. Sturdy houses will go up. Above all, more land will be cleared and planted. We shall not starve again!"

There was some applause at these bright prospects. But on the whole the one hundred sixty new arrivals, the one hundred fifty men, women, and children from Bermuda, the few survivors from the Starving Time, were uneasy. They wondered, as I did, how all this could be accomplished.

Lord De La Warr was quick to give the answer. "We shall work six hours each day of the week, save Sunday. Furthermore, no one, not even the gentlemen, shall be exempt from work. Those whose breeding has not acquainted them with the saw, the pick, the ax, and the hammer shall be introduced to the same."

The "gentlemen" were silent. The footmen and body-servants hired by the gentlemen to attend them were also silent. It was a scene much like the one in Bermuda when Governor Gates had harangued the crowd. And with the same effect.

Six of the new gentlemen and six from Francis Pearepoint's Bermuda group were sent to the mouth of the river, which teemed with every variety of fish. After two days they came back with empty baskets, having failed to cast a single hook.

The rebuilding of the church and the bulwarks dragged, as did work on the huts and the fort. Fort Charles and Fort Henry were never started. Fields lay uncleared and untilled. Indians watched from the tall marsh grass, from bush and tree.

After some months Lord De La Warr fell ill and decided to return to England. He complained of weakness of the limbs, but I believe he had foreseen that this Supply, like the First and Second Supplies, would fail. Winter had found the garrison without adequate food or shelter. And the failure would be blamed squarely upon him.

Lord De La Warr's decision gave me a chance to return to England. I hadn't spoken a word to him during his months in Jamestown, but I had met him at the Foxcroft masque, when he made a passing comment about my pretty blue dress.

I went to talk to him once I heard of his decision and took Humility with me.

He had kept himself apart from the fort, living and directing the colony's affairs from his flagship. His cabin was twice the size of Admiral Somers' cabin on the *Sea Venture*, all paneled in precious woods, with golden scrolls around the doors and a ceiling covered with scenes of Neptune and his court of sea nymphs sporting among the waves.

A small man, he looked even smaller now. He had shrunk since the day he stepped ashore at Jamestown in his large white ruff and slashed red velvet.

He sat at a big table, half-hidden behind a pyramid of charts and papers. He didn't rise as I came in or ask me to sit in one of his damask chairs. Nor did he do so when I introduced myself and reminded him that we had met at the Foxcroft masque.

"Oh, yes, to raise funds for the Virginia venture," he said scornfully. "What a hapless occasion! Little did we know what a calamity we were bringing down upon ourselves. What laughter we would evoke among our enemies, the Spaniards! What turmoil lay in store. The impoverishment of many who financed the folly. The deaths of lordly reputations."

"And the deaths of many people," I said.

He peered at me over the pyramid of charts, his eyes cold, as if I were to blame for Jamestown. The tide was running and the flagship strained against the ropes that held her to the trees. I thought that she, too, was anxious to leave Jamestown.

"Why are you here," he asked me, "instead of at work?"

He was angry before I had a chance to say a word. It was a bad beginning.

"I wish to go with your ship when you return to England."

Lord De La Warr got to his feet as if to dismiss me, tottered, grasped his chair, and sat down again.

"Back to England? To England!" he shouted in a weak voice. "What an outlandish idea! You're sorely needed here, young woman."

"But, sir, you just said that Jamestown's a calamity. That our enemies, the Spaniards, are laughing at us."

He sighed. "Words spoken in a weak moment. Jamestown will persist and flourish. As soon as I return to London, I'll see that a hardened soldier is sent out to take my place. Someone who has been in battle. Someone who can handle the shiftless and tame the unruly, deliver a bloody nose or spring the gallows trap, whatever the offense demands. Someone with a stronger stomach than I have. Above all, a man who will see the Indian for what he really is—a treacherous barbarian—and treat him as such."

"Sir, I have this child to look after. She's one of the three children who survived the Starving Time. All of them are ill. They can't possibly last another winter, even if you send a soldier who can tame the unruly and kill the Indians."

"Who is your husband? Where is he? Bring him here. I have a word for him. The child?"

"I am unmarried, sir, and the girl's name is Humility Pryor. Admiral Somers had made me her guardian until we get to England."

Humility was hidden from him behind the vast desk. I brought her forward to the center of the cabin where he could see the face that seemed all eyes and the arms and legs that looked like sticks.

"Children are needed here in Jamestown," he said. "They're the heart of the future. Don't worry, she'll be taken care of when our new leader arrives." He paused. "By the way, you signed a legal contract before you boarded the ship in Plymouth, did you not?"

"By happenstance, sir. I sold shares at the Foxcroft masque, you may remember, but I never intended to come to Jamestown. Jamestown was far from my thoughts."

The cold look in De La Warr's eyes disappeared, or was it a shaft of sunlight that suddenly came through the windows?

"I remember now," he said. "You were madly in love with Anthony Foxcroft and followed him to Plymouth. Tongues wagged. It was a scandal. To Plymouth and beyond. To Bermuda. I've heard that he was lost at sea."

Suddenly there burst upon us a frightened solider who announced that hostiles were lurking on the river. "Three canoes," he said, "carrying what look to be six warriors painted red and black. One of them has a gun, which he shot at us. Struck Sir William Poses in the arm. We can overtake them, sir. They're going slow."

"In what direction?"

"Upriver."

"Let them proceed."

"But, sir, they're—"

Lord De La Warr waved him out of the cabin.

Waiting to come in was the cook. When the lord told an attendant to shut the door, the cook said through the crack, "Weevils in the corn, sir."

"Sort them out," De La Warr said.

"Hundreds, sir."

"Sort out what you can," De La Warr said, turning his cold eyes upon me. "And now you wish to return to England. A busy young lady, heh? You have a child to take care of. What else?"

"The king has asked me to help the queen with Her Majesty's correspondence."

De La Warr corrected me. "The king does not ask. The king commands. And if he has commanded you to join his household as a secretary to the queen, he has not taken kindly to your running off after Foxcroft. Should you now appear in London, the king might toss you in the Tower, cool you off a bit."

He squinted his tired blue eyes. "Secretary to Queen Anne? It is most unlikely. But the king *is* given to lightsome jokes."

To prove that I was not lying, I took off the ring and laid it on the desk.

He picked it up and ran a finger over the coiled serpent.

"The ring is a gift from the king," I said. "I was wearing it the day he asked me to go to London and serve the queen."

"You can serve the queen in Jamestown," he said, handing the ring back to me, "but you can't do so if you're a Jamestown deserter. The king has lofty dreams for the New World. His Majesty would not take kindly to someone who's fled the land."

Unsteady on his thin legs, Lord De La Warr showed us to the deck. The big ship strained at her moorings. Desperately I sought for words that would sway him.

Beyond him the river gleamed. A cannon roared and an iron ball struck the water, far short of a line of canoes moving toward the distant shore. Indians were everywhere, on the river, among the trees of the forest. They watched from the tall grass and the salt meadows. They watched night and day.

"This is no place for a child," I said loudly. "Nor for anyone else."

Lord De La Warr looked me in the eye. "Only for the brave," he answered, and closed the cabin door behind us.

At dusk I took Humility by the hand and went back to the

ship. The sailors were eating their supper, laughing, happy to be leaving Jamestown.

The ship, except for De La Warr's cabin, was much like the *Deliverance*. I took Humility down a ladder-way to the bilge. At the stern I found a cubbyhole where tattered sails were stored. We got inside, closed the door, and stretched out on the sails.

The hole smelled of tar and turpentine and was so dark we could scarcely see each other. We had no food or water, but that did not matter. De La Warr planned to sail at dawn on the ebbing tide. By noon we would be across Chesapeake Bay, bound for England. Then, when it was too late to turn back, Humility and I would appear on deck.

I cautioned her to be quiet. "Do not talk aloud. If you have anything to say, whisper. Better yet, remain silent."

Everything worked well for a time, albeit she was bursting with excitement. By a slit in the door that let in a sliver of light, I could see her eyes shining. She pressed my hand. We were conspirators in league against the world's awful things. We listened to the sound of sailors on the deck, to those in the rigging, to the voices on shore bidding the ship farewell.

I saw the glint of two small eyes before Humility did. We were lying on coils of rope. The eyes shone out from the folds of a tattered sail. In the dim light they looked like beautiful gems, like twin rubies.

With one hand I quietly opened the door and with the other shook the sail. It was a mistake. I should have done nothing. The rat was at home among the canvas folds. At my rash act, it scurried across Humility's chest, down a leg, over a foot, and out the door.

Her screams followed it. I closed the door and took her in my arms and waited. I didn't wait long. I heard running steps. Then the door flew open and a bewhiskered young man stood staring down at us.

"Behold," he said with some surprise. "What do we have here?"

"Stowaways," I said weakly.

"Upon my word, upon Poseidon's golden spear," he said, "if it's not Serena Lynn and little Humility!"

I recognized him. He was an assistant to Lord De La Warr. "Mr. Bertram," I said, "please close the door and let us be."

Mr. Bertram pondered. He stuck out his tongue and wet his lips. I believe that he would have closed the door and gone his way had it not been for the two sailors who came at that instant for the coil of rope we were sitting upon.

As it was, he helped us to our feet, escorted us to the gangplank, and waved us good-bye.

Twenty

Lord De La Warr sailed from Jamestown the next day. I watched his ship leave the riverbank while drummers beat on their flag-draped drums, himself propped against a bulwark, waving his braided hat. It was a bitter sight to see the ship gaily disappear in the morning haze, alas, without me. Yet it only strengthened my resolve to leave Jamestown. There would be other chances, other ships that sailed for England.

A chance seemed to come sooner than I expected. Lord De La Warr had left his kinsman, Sir George Percy, in charge of the colony. In desperation, Sir George decided once more to try to find Pocahontas.

He sent forth three bands of scouts to search her out. One band went up the James to the mountains where it began. Another searched the Pamunkey River, still another the land of the Nansemonds. All returned with wildly conflicting stories.

Pocahontas had quarreled with her father and fled after I left Werowocómoco. Her father was interested in improving trade with the Patawamake, members of his confederacy, and had sent her north as an agent of good will. She was not an agent but had gone to live with the Rappahannocks because she had married one of their young men.

Sir George was confused, so confused that he did nothing. This was another bitter disappointment. I bided my time.

In May, Captain Argall, who had ferried De La Warr back to England, sailed up the river with a fleet of six tall ships and a warrior to take the colony from Percy's faltering hands.

The new leader was Sir Thomas Dale, a general who had gained a reputation for bravery in the Flanders War. He strode ashore surrounded by fifty liveried attendants, much as Lord De La Warr had before him. But there was a difference in his measured steps and the fiery glances he cast to right and left.

"He's been warned," Tom Barlow said. "He's been told about the First Supply fleet and the Second Supply. And Lord De La Warr has told him what happened to the Third. He knows now what to look for."

Dale was an imposing figure, long in the legs, broad in the chest, florid-faced, with a blunt chin half-hidden in a starched white ruff.

"He looks determined," Tom Barlow said. "That's good. De La Warr had to give up before he ever got started. There's hope, I think."

I had few predictions or hopes concerning Sir Thomas Dale and what he could or would do to save the perishing colony, though I was most certain he'd fail as the others had failed—that hundreds of colonists would die as they had died in the past. Yet I did have one consuming thought. It was that Humility and I would not be among the dead!

We followed Sir Thomas and the three hundred new-comers to higher ground where the church had stood.

He gave no speech and refused the Reverend Bucke when prayer was suggested. He strode through the ashes of the five-cornered garrison, talking to himself, then repaired to his flagship and was not seen for days.

Rumors spread. Appalled by what he had seen, Sir Thomas had given up. He was making ready to leave for London. But on the third day he reappeared and called everyone together. In a short proclamation, reading quickly in thin but arrogant tones, he imposed martial law upon the colony.

Death was the penalty for disrespect to the king or his representatives. Thieves would be branded or have an ear lopped off. Those who robbed the house where food was stored could expect to be tied to a tree and left to starve. Deserters would be burned, broken upon the wheel (he had brought a wheel with him), staked out in the weather, or shot.

The lord marshal's laws were strictly carried out.

By summer, all the laws had been broken and all of the culprits punished, including Francis Pearepoint, gentleman, who lost an ear for announcing that he had signed a contract to search for treasure, not to wield a hoe. And Emma Swinton, who was tied to a tree and forced to stay a week in rain and shine, in an effort to silence her clacking tongue and dire predictions.

The laws of Marshal Dale became known as the Laws of Blood. Yet good things came out of this reign of terror.

Deciding that Jamestown was located in an unhealthy place that was very difficult to defend against Indians or Spanish raiders, he began a town some miles up the James, which he called Henrico, in honor of noble Prince Henry. Carpenters worked day and night to build it.

The new town lay on a high bluff beside the river, surrounded on three sides by the richest of farmland. Tom Barlow was one of the first to apply for land and the second, after John Rolfe, to receive a parcel, a small one beside a pretty stream that ran quietly into the James through a grove of yellow pines.

Tom cut down trees and, with the help of neighbors whom he promised to help later on, built a one-room cabin with a stone fireplace ten feet wide. The men built it in a week, working on Sunday, which distressed Tom greatly.

He came down the river in his canoe and invited everyone at the fort to partake in a housewarming. Emma Swinton and Humility and I were the only ones from the fort who came.

It was a cloudless day. Wildflowers were blooming on the land Tom hadn't yet tilled and the air smelled of them and yellow pines.

We stood outside the cabin, the three of us from the fort and several soon-to-be neighbors who were working on another cabin in Henrico. Tom read something from the Bible, we all prayed, and then we went inside. I gasped and exclaimed how beautiful it was, the way the pine logs fit together so snugly.

"The fireplace's big enough to roast a whole deer," I said to please Tom, who was perspiring with pleasure.

"You'll not do much cooking without a trestle and some tongs and big iron pots," Emma Swinton said.

"Those will come later," Tom said. "Maybe soon, with the next supply ships."

"If you're alive by then," Emma said. "I heard Indians when we were outside. Hiding in the trees somewhere."

"They're curious."

"Waiting," Emma said, twisting her mouth.

"To make friends," Tom said.

"Waiting for the right time to scalp you and burn your cabin down," Emma said.

Tom smiled and pointed to a musket sitting in a corner, "I'm ready, and everyone in Henrico will be ready," he said, "and the Indians know it."

Cheers went up from seven men. Their wives, I noticed, were silent.

Tom served the currant cake I had made and a jug of milk the others brought. A young man played a harmonica and Tom played his viola, but nobody danced except Humility and me. The rest, being mostly members of a strange sect that thought dancing sinful, looked on with disapproval.

A little later, the Henrico people trooped off through the woods together, the men shouldering their primed firelocks. Emma, Humility, and I went down to the canoe.

But just before we pulled away, I remembered I had left my cake pan, the only pan I owned, behind. I slipped out of the canoe and ran back to get it. As I came out of the cabin, holding the heavy pan across my chest, Tom was by the door.

"You look pretty in the doorway," he said, "with the sun bright and shining in your hair. But you look pretty anywhere, rain or shine."

I closed the door and started off down the path that led to the river. Tom took the pan and fell in step beside me.

"We've known each other for some time," he said, taking a dozen steps to say these few words. "I've been thinking, since the cabin is finished and everything's ready except a few pots and things, that it would be fine for us to be man and wife together."

We were nearing the river. I took the pan from him and was silent.

"I guess it's a surprise," Tom said, "my speaking this way."

I was not surprised. He'd been thinking about marriage for a long time, not just since the cabin was finished. Since we landed in Jamestown. Before that, in Bermuda. And perhaps even before that, on the ship. The cabin gave him the courage to speak.

"You don't have to give your answer today," he said.

Twenty-one

O nce the rebuilding of Jamestown and the building of
   Henrico were well under way, Marshal Dale acted
swiftly in the search for Pocahontas.

During the winter, he had read the reports Governor
Percy had gathered. He was certain that she was living
somewhere on the Potomac River or one of its tributaries.
Why she was there did not matter, nor whether she wanted
to return to Jamestown. What mattered was that she be
found as quickly as possible and reunited with her father
before the storehouses ran dry and the colony starved.

He called Captain Argall and me to the fort, which he had
rebuilt and armed with rows of cannons. We reached his
quarters by a long flight of steps in the shape of a corkscrew
and came out breathless, into a large room stuffed with
armor. The walls were decorated with crossed swords and
flags, mementos of Marshal Dale's campaign in Flanders.

We found him standing at a small window, really a
gunport, looking down upon the river and Captain Argall's
ship.

"You were on the Potomac only a few months ago," he

said to the captain. "And before that, sent by Lord De La Warr. Both times you were treated well?"

"Yes, and fortunate in making the acquaintance of Japazaws, king of Pastancie. The king was well disposed toward me because years ago he was befriended by Captain John Smith. It was the reputation of Smith among the Patawamake that made it possible to bring back eleven hundred bushels of splendid corn."

"Unfortunately gone, consumed weeks ago," said Dale. "You also brought three hostages and left one with Japazaws, an Ensign Swift, as proof of good will. But more important, you brought news of Pocahontas."

"Rumors."

"But believable ones."

"At least a shadow of the truth," Captain Argall said. "She's somewhere in the vicinity, possibly on one of the creeks, but not on the river, because I was there. The Indians along the creeks are extremely dangerous."

"Can you navigate the creeks?" Dale asked.

"Not in the *Treasurer*. She draws close to nine feet. But I could if I carried a longboat."

"When can you sail? The earliest? As you know, our storehouses are almost empty."

"There's a leak to attend. A list to the mainmast. Work on the rudder. This is Monday. Say in a week."

"Kindly get at it," Thomas Dale said. He waited until Argall had left, standing at the gunport until he saw him climb the ship's ladder, before he spoke to me.

"I have called you," he said, "because I hear that you have met and talked to Pocahontas. Is that right?"

"Yes, sir. At the Powhatan temple in Werowocómoco."

He gave me a dubious glance. "From what I heard of your trip I expected to find an experienced woman. But before me stands a mere maiden. How old are you?"

"Nineteen, sir."

"God befriend me! This is not a frolicsome day in the country, an English picnic. This is an Indian mission fraught with danger, as Captain Argall testified."

"No more dangerous than life in Jamestown," I replied, fearful that my chances had slipped away. "Captain Argall sailed the Potomac twice and has told us that he was well treated there."

"Captain Argall was on a different mission. He was trading beads and bells for food. This has nothing to do with trade. We are on a search in strange waters. Our quarry is a proud, headstrong girl protected by powerful friends. She can't be captured by force and hauled away to Jamestown. She must be persuaded, ever so gently, to join us."

"I agree. I'll talk to her gently and kindly."

"In what, the King's English?"

"She does speak some English, sir. But since that time, I have studied some of the Indian dialects. There are six captives here at the fort and I've learned from them."

Marshal Dale looked impressed. To further impress him, I added, "Also some of the languages spoken around the Potomac, like those used by the Susquehanna and the Masgawameke."

"Quite remarkable," the marshal said. "And no doubt you've learned the sign language, which I understand is common among the various tribes."

Eagerly I made the signs of clouds, the sun, the moon, a voyage of five days, a pretty girl, and a tall, ugly man. I would have made more signs if the marshal had not broken in to say that with some trepidation he would accept me as a member of the Argall party.

"But mind you," he warned, "Captain Argall is a disciplinarian. He'll brook no female vapors. I repeat, this is a most dangerous undertaking. And you must think of it as such, not as a girlish prank."

"Oh, the good Lord forbid it, it is no prank, Your Honor. It is a most serious undertaking."

"De La Warr told me when we last talked in London that you were a heedless sort. I am inclined to believe him right. Therefore a word of caution before you set off. A lively sense of fear has saved many lives. And it could well save yours, Miss Serena."

Fear? Fear, as always, was far from my thoughts, but I frowned, nodded, and said, "I'll remember your words. I'll be fearful, Marshal Dale."

Striding to the gunport, he watched the men idling on the deck of Argall's ship. After a moment he shouted down, "Stir your stumps, rascal outcasts, or I'll see that the captain is promptly among you with a cat-o'-nine-tails."

He turned his angry gaze upon me, half-smiled as he saw my beaming face, then suddenly shook his head. "It won't do," he said. "An unfortunate idea. I would be dismantled limb from limb if you were killed. It's a man's job. It requires a firm hand and a cold eye. We deal with savages, not with the civilized. Indians understand only the sword. They cower in their dens now that I have used it upon them."

They did cower. Along the James and its streams, throughout Southern Tidewater, Dale was known as a bloody monster. There was scarcely a family among Powhatan's people that did not mourn a brother, a husband, or a father, someone he had tortured or killed. The laws he used upon the Indians were even more ferocious than the Laws of Blood with which he ruled Jamestown.

I saw that my dream, my chance of returning to England, was slipping away. It made me angry. "You don't need a man with a sword and a cold eye to bring Pocahontas back to Jamestown."

"Something tells me she won't return without them."

"From what Captain John Smith has said about her and

from what I have learned, she will not return if she's ill-treated."

"We don't need to ill-treat her. If she resists, we'll take her firmly by the hand."

"And bring her here against her will? 'Tis nonsensical, sir."

The scar across his forehead turned dead-white. It was a warning, but I did not heed it.

"You'll have a sullen girl on your hands. Who, if I know her, will not lift her little finger to put so much as a grain of corn in your empty storehouses."

"You know more about her than you do about Marshal Thomas Dale."

"Yes, much more. She is like me, I found. She won't be threatened."

"Marshal Dale does not threaten. He acts, as you well know."

"You can't force her into anything, no more than her father could. She was Captain John Smith's dear friend. Her father objected to their friendship. She defied him. She saw Captain Smith whenever it pleased her. Pocahontas and I are nearly the same age. We are alike in many ways. We have talked together. We can again."

The marshal began to stride, his boots pounding on the floor, his sword clanking at his side. He glanced out the window, shouted something, and fixed me with a sidelong stare.

"You're mother to a child, a solemn, pale-faced little thing. Have you made provisions to care for her if you go?"

"No, but I shall, this day."

"I repeat again, 'tis a dangerous mission you embark upon. If you're captured and slain in some heathenish rite, I will see that she's properly taken care of."

Heathenish rite? Death? It was a sobering thought, yet it passed quickly.

"Gather yourself," he said. "Be ready to sail within a fortnight."

"I am ready now," I said in a firm voice. "And if I don't return, will you take proper care of Humility?"

"A promise."

"And send her to England?"

"Yes, to England."

"To Foxcroft?"

"To Foxcroft, which I knew well before you were born."

Twenty-two

Captain Argall, working his crew around the clock, driven by Marshal Dale, had his ship ready to sail at noon on Monday of the following week. Marshal Dale sent us off with a fiery speech.

"Remember," he said from the riverbank, resplendent in his marshal's uniform, "that you go on a voyage fraught with the gravest dangers, one that must not fail. The life of the colony, its existence, depends upon you. Remember that a captive girl brought Naman to the Prophet. A captive woman was the instrument by which Iberia was brought into the Christian fold. You'll be faced by the devil's vast minions, you who are so few. But remember that God gives the weak of his world the strength to confound the mighty."

Humility stood beside him, clutching the hem of his velvet cloak. At the last minute he had demanded that I permit him to care for her while I was gone. She was in safe hands. Still I wondered if he'd spoil her, if she'd be bedazzled by his glittering sword, jeweled chains, and loops of gold braid, by bits of food taken from the barren storehouse.

We took Quemo, the Patawamake hostage, with us. The

day was hot. The shores of the Chesapeake were lost in haze, but a brisk south wind filled our sails and drove us hard through the night. We were becalmed the next day in an airless maze of isles and inlets.

There was fear among some members of the crew, Marshal Dale's warning still ringing in their ears, that we might be ambushed in one of the narrow passages. But Captain Argall assured them that the Indians in this part of the Chesapeake were friendly.

"I've made the voyage twice before," he said, "and found them well disposed toward the white man."

A tall, powerfully built man with a steady eye, a captain thoroughly familiar with the ocean seas and the Virginia waters, he lessened their fears. But the next day, as we passed close upon the shores of a wooded island, not an Indian to be seen, a shower of stone-tipped arrows descended upon us. Three of our men were wounded and one was pierced through the heart.

We entered peaceful waters on the fourth day under a deep blue sky, a beautiful forest marching down to the shore and the air loud with bird cries. But here, too, there was a sudden alarm.

Coming upon a break in the forest on the landward side of the bay, the lookout called down from the mainmast that he saw what looked like an encampment of a thousand Indians. As we drew closer, we saw that it was a great herd of shaggy beasts grazing along the grassy banks of a stream, animals Captain Argall said were buffalo.

At sunset of the following day we came to Pastancie, a sizable Indian village set back from the river upon a low bluff, where supper fires were alight. Captain Argall instructed the crew to lower a longboat and called three of his officers to the deck.

"You were here with me before," he told them. "You have talked to Japazaws, the king of Pastancie. Talk to him again and tell him that I have reason to believe that Pocahontas lives in this kingdom. And I demand that he talk to his brother, King Patowomek, and tell him to deliver her up to me. Along with Ensign Swift, who was left here as a hostage, as well as a goodly burden of corn. Unless he acts promptly, I shall put him down as an enemy and treat him and his people accordingly."

On the voyage from Jamestown, Captain Argall had shown me measured courtesy, yet I gained the feeling that I would not be on the ship if Marshal Dale had not insisted. Furthermore, I gathered that he had no thought of using me to persuade Pocahontas to return to Jamestown. This accomplishment, this coup, he wished to bring about himself, without any help from me.

"I was sent here by Marshal Dale," I said before Argall had finished with his instructions. "To demand that King Patowomek deliver Pocahontas to you means that she will be brought here against her will, as a captive. It's possible that the king will refuse your demands. In which case you will have a deadly enemy, and the prize you came for will have fled in terror."

Captain Argall, surprised by my outburst, strode to the rail and thought for a while.

He was not a ninny. He was probably having doubts about his strict demands on Patowomek. What if the king did refuse to deliver the girl? Would he have a bitter enemy on his hands? What if Pocahontas did flee in terror? And what would Marshal Dale say to him if he returned to Jamestown empty-handed?

He decided to meet me partway. He told the officers to make no demands upon the king, and to escort Japazaws to the ship, leaving Ensign Swift behind.

They came back in a short time with Japazaws and his wife. She was a tall, handsome woman dressed in bleached deerhide and copper bangles and earrings. Japazaws was half her size and ugly, but with a winning smile that puckered his face from chin to forehead.

Captain Argall clasped him tightly, though Japazaws gleamed with grease, and said, "My brother, tell me truthfully, is the daughter of Powhatan among you?"

Japazaws smiled but did not answer. His wife, making a wild sound with the copper loops in her ears, nodded.

"Convey to the princess my warmest greetings," Captain Argall said, looking from one to the other, wisely addressing both of them.

Japazaws smiled again and his wife nodded. The captain was speaking English. I wondered if they understood any of it.

"And kindly ask the princess," he said, "if she will honor His Majesty's servants by having food with them on board His Majesty's ship some afternoon at her convenience."

Japazaws' wife made signs that she would give his words to the princess. They both lingered until Captain Argall gave each a gift of beads.

When three days passed and nothing was seen of them, Argall became anxious, then angry. He put the ship's crew on alert and primed the cannon. Although he said nothing to me, I concluded that the party for Pocahontas was a ruse. Once she was aboard the ship, he planned to seize her, quell her cries, and sail off for Jamestown. It was a foolish idea but I kept silent.

On the fifth day, Japazaws and his wife appeared with an interpreter. He spoke to Captain Argall in his native dialect, and the interpreter translated the words into Algonquian, which I passed on to Captain Argall as best I could.

"I gave your message to the Council of Elders," Japazaws said, smiling, puckering his face. "And they are talking together with Pocahontas."

Captain Argall had been pacing the deck, barely holding

back anger that had been simmering now for five anxious days. At the news that his message to Pocahontas had been turned over to a Council of Elders, he quit pacing.

"What has a gaggle of old men to do with the proud daughter of the mighty Powhatan?" he sputtered. "Is she a captive, a slave, a helpless toy, not allowed to make up her own mind, treated in such a humiliating fashion?"

A setting sun shimmered on the deck. Smoke drifted out from the village and settled around us.

Japazaws' wife was wearing a heavy robe trimmed with raccoon fur. She took it off and stood in her scanty shift, looking at Argall. She didn't wait for his outburst to be translated. She gauged the depths of his anger. She had already gauged his interest in the girl. He had come a long way to find her, and was not here just to talk.

She studied him over the edge of her turkey-feather fan. "The Elders will talk," she said. "Days will pass."

"How many days?" Captain Argall said.

"If they talk, the days of summer will pass."

Captain Argall grasped his beard in frustration. Visible over the edge of her fan, her black eyes slowly closed upon the scene. She opened them again and pointed to a bangle he wore around his neck. A large ruby clasped in the mouth of a leopard hung from a gold chain. After making a motion to her own neck, she pointed toward the village, then to the spot where she stood.

Her message was clear. For Argall's ruby and chain she would deliver Pocahontas to the ship.

"When?" the captain exclaimed.

She held up two fingers and pointed to the sun.

Still frustrated, preferring to send her packing and to rely instead upon his cannon, the captain nodded. Whereupon Japazaws smilingly pointed at the sword Argall wore. Argall slipped it from its scabbard. For a moment I thought he meant to run the Indian through, but he relented and passed the weapon over.

With necklace and sword, Japazaws and his wife left the ship and paddled happily away in the dusk, taking the interpreter with them.

From the village came cries of wonder and delight at their return. Fires leaped up, streaking the forest and the river; drums beat. We waited for the two days to pass. They passed but the village was silent. There was no sign of Japazaws, his wife, and the princess.

On the morning of the third day, Captain Argall called together the crew and the sixteen soldiers of the guard and laid plans for an attack upon the King Patowomek. The crew was to remain on the ship to man the cannon, to be ready if necessary to move out of danger. The guards were to slip ashore at midnight, attack the village of Pastancie, and seize the helpless quarry.

I objected to his plans in the same words and spirit as before, but Captain Argall turned a deaf ear to my pleadings. A violent rainstorm, which burst upon us at nightfall, sweeping away one of our small boats, did what I was unable to do. It caused Captain Argall to delay the attack until the next night.

In the morning, before the bugler announced the day and the first breakfast fires showed in the village, I slipped away in a small boat tied to the ship.

Twenty-three

The village of Pastancie sat back from a low bluff above the river. To reach it I followed a trail flooded with water from the night's storm. Below me the ship's crew was gathering on the deck, and Captain Argall stood in their midst. There was no sign that he knew I had left.

As I came to the head of the trail, I smelled smoke and cooking food and heard the sound of quiet voices. But as I approached the village, dogs began to bark. Then suddenly a sparsely clad group of warriors surrounded me. Their faces were painted with streaks of white and black. Down their legs ran red snakelike patterns. Weasel skins hung from their belts and they had long spears tufted with feathers.

A man carrying a battered gun spoke to me in Algonquian, most of which I understood, and at the same time made gestures, which I fully understood.

"You have come from Jamestown," he said, pointing down the Potomac River, toward Chesapeake Bay and beyond. "For two days I saw you coming. I understand you come in peace. But I do not see my friend, Quemo. Is Quemo dead?"

A hissing sound passed from one to another among his warriors. Spears rattled.

"Quemo," I said, "is on the ship."

"I have seen the ship, but not my friend Quemo."

"He is on the ship. The captain will bring him."

"When?"

"Soon."

The hissing sound grew louder.

"Today," I said with a gesture toward the sun.

"Why are you here?" the chieftain asked. "What do you wish?"

"I wish to talk to Pocahontas."

The chieftain gave me a sharp look. "I see no beads, no copper, no pans, no nothing."

It was foolish of me to come here without presents.

The chieftain glanced at his warriors, at each of them, and shrugged his shoulders in disgust.

"The captain has many presents," I said. "He will bring them."

"Today?"

"Today."

What if Captain Argall brought death instead of beads? I envisioned myself a hostage. I might be held for weeks, months, a year, perhaps.

The chieftain pointed down a crooked street, to the far end where a long house stood. "King Japazaws," he said. "You will talk to him about Pocahontas."

He said something that I did not understand and bowed, but he was not happy. Huts lined both sides of the street that led to the long house. Pine fires were burning in front of the huts and smoke that stung the eyes made it hard to see.

Before we had gone far, a girl emerged from the pall of smoke and came quickly toward us. By the way she held her head, the curtain of black hair, I knew who it was. I greeted her in English and she answered me in English, speaking slowly, running her words together; yet I understood her, as I had before.

"I saw you from the bluff," she said. "You were on the ship. I waved to you. You did not wave back."

"Because I didn't see you," I said. "I would have waved. I came a long way to talk to you again."

She looked at me intently. Her eyes were as I remembered them—deep-set, wide apart, and very dark, neither friendly nor unfriendly. From the many rumors about her, I had decided that she was here on the Potomac to hide from her father's wrath. I had made up a message that he had forgiven her and that he begged his dearest child to return to his kingdom. This was a lie. Meeting her gaze, I could not tell it.

"What talk," she asked, "did you come with?"

I hesitated. I had come for one purpose. As quickly as possible, before Captain Argall could commit some rash act, I had to get her safely on the ship.

"You come to talk about the invitation?" she said, and paused, searching for words, making a vague gesture.

"Yes, can you come?"

"The Elders talk, lots of talk."

"But you are a princess," I said. "The daughter of an emperor. You can do what you wish."

A light kindled in her eyes, as if she had forgotten who she was and suddenly realized that a princess did not wait for Elders to decide what she should or should not do.

By now we were surrounded by a mass of women, children, and yelping dogs. The men, likely, had armed themselves and gone off to guard the trail to the river. Captain Argall would have long since discovered I had gone. It would be clear to him that I was in the village. It would not be long before he gathered his soldiers and followed me.

"The ship, what is its name?" she asked.

"Treasurer."

The word meant nothing to her.

"It is bigger than Captain Smith's ship," she said. "I walked on his ship." Her gaze wandered off, as though she were reliving a happier time. She smiled. "I would like to walk on this ship." Then she brightened, held up a finger, and pointed at the sun. "Tomorrow."

"Today is better," I said, aware that "tomorrow" in Indian fashion could mean a week. In that time there was no telling what Captain Argall, angered by the delay, might do. Again, fearing the worst, I told her that any day, possibly tomorrow, the *Treasurer* might sail away.

I don't know that she understood me. She was silent for a while. Then she spoke to a woman standing nearby who left and quickly returned with a feathered cloak and a headdress of beads and fur.

It was a signal for a procession to leave the long house.

Behind musicians making an awful din and a group of old men whom I took to be the Council of Elders was Japazaws' tall wife and Japazaws running along beside her. The procession gathered us up, and to the tooting of horns and the beating of wooden clackers, we swept out of the village and down the trail. It was all done in such an orderly fashion that I began to wonder. Had Japazaws planned the procession? Had Pocahontas made up her mind to visit the ship before I even talked to her?

Halfway down the river trail we met Captain Argall and a band of soldiers dressed in armor and carrying weapons. It was an awkward moment. He took in the scene at a glance and ordered his troops to turn about.

We followed them to the river, where the soldiers aligned themselves in two rows, forming an aisle. Pocahontas, Japazaws, his wife, and their retainers passed through it regally and were helped into a longboat. We all were rowed to the ship.

It was a hot morning, with the sun slanting straight down and steam rising from the river. Captain Argall had an awning stretched over the foredeck for the comfort of his guests. Jugs of a pink drink were served. Pocahontas took a sip of hers, made a wry face, walked to the rail, spat it into the river, and wandered off.

She stopped at the mainmast and looked up at the ladder that soared high overhead to the crow's nest. Remembering Captain Smith's descriptions of how she swung in the Jamestown trees, jumped the palisade walls, swam the wide James River, I half expected her to set off and climb the ladder. She did put a foot on the first rung, then turned away with a heavy sigh.

As she walked toward the stern, Japazaws jumped to his feet and pursued her. Climbing the steps of the sterncastle, they were lost to view. At once Japazaws' wife confronted Captain Argall.

She wore his ruby and chain. One of the crew passed by at this moment with a copper kettle. She pointed at this and made a motion, a quick jab of her thumb, toward the shore. Her signs were clear. They had completed their part of the bargain. They had delivered Pocahontas to the ship. They wished to be gone.

Captain Argall had been loath to surrender his ruby and even more unhappy to give up his sword. The copper kettle was of no consequence. But with the show of greatest reluctance, he handed it over.

When Japazaws and the princess returned to our circle, Captain Argall took her hand and escorted her to the gunnery room. As soon as the gunnery door had closed, the Japazaws climbed over the side and were rowed ashore.

Long before the king and his wife were out of sight, the anchors were pulled in, and the ship nosed slowly downstream. We had not moved beyond the first bend in the river when Pocahontas appeared at the sterncastle door. She was nearly as tall as Captain Argall, who stood behind her. Her broad shoulders filled the doorway.

As she ran to the sterncastle rail, I hurried up the ladder and stood beside her. I feared that, seeing that the ship was bearing her away from Pastancie, she might be tempted to throw herself into the river and swim ashore.

She held tight to the rail, her body tense. In one swift leap she could reach the river. The water was calm and the shore close upon us. Long before the ship could be turned about and a boat lowered, she would be on shore. The forest, which came to the riverbank, would hide her. We would never see her again.

"You'll be happier in Jamestown," I said, grasping her arm.

She pulled away. She said nothing. Her gaze was fixed on the shore and the forest.

"Stay," I said. "I'll protect you. Stay. You'll not be harmed."

She turned to face me. She was still silent. But in her eyes was a look that made me wonder if she was not glad to be leaving the kingdom of Patowomek.

Captain Argall did all he could to make her comfortable. He lodged her in the gunnery room, the best place on the ship save his own cabin. He instructed the crew to treat her with deference at all times.

She liked their attention and the ship, which she roamed from bow to sterncastle. She liked her new life so much that, as we sailed back to Jamestown, I began to believe that she had outwitted us all, that for a long time she had yearned to go home and make peace with her father. The kidnapping had come to her as a wonderful surprise.

We talked about England, I think because John Smith was there.

She wanted to know what the English people did, what

they ate, what games they played. She was sad when I told her I was going back to England.

One morning she said, "We speak like friends, but I do not know your name."

"Serena Lynn."

"It sounds like a bird singing," she said.

We were in the gunnery room and she was braiding her hair. It fell to her waist, coarse as a horse's tail but alive and lustrous. When I saw her in the temple, her hair had covered most of her face. I hadn't seen that it was cropped short in front and on the sides, a sign that she was still unwed.

"Serena Lynn," she said, trilling the words. "What does it mean?"

"Nothing that I know about. It's just a name. What does Pocahontas mean?"

"My father gave it to me. It means Bright Stream Between Two Hills. Do you like it?"

"It is beautiful," I said. "It fits you. To me you *are* a bright stream." I didn't say that I liked it better than the name Pocahontas, which always sounded lumpy to me, like a wagon bumping along a rough road.

She paused and turned her head to look at me. We looked at each other in silence, like two travelers who have come upon each other unexpectedly out of a dark forest.

"I like you," she said. "I hope you like me."

"I do, Bright Stream. From the bottom of my heart, I do."

"Would you like to know my secret name?" she asked. Before I could answer, she said, "It is Matoax. It means Snow Feather."

She had braided her hair and piled it on top of her head. She looked a little like one of our Jamestown ladies. But then she got out her leather shift and put on a snow-white mantle trimmed with swan's down and, about her neck, double loops of white pearls. She looked like a snow feather now, nothing like one of the plain ladies of Jamestown.

It was April and warm. We went out on the deck. We were near the village where the Indians had attacked the ship before. As we came abreast of the place, we were met by a shower of arrows, some of which whistled close above us. In return, two of the ship's cannons answered with shots that set the village afire.

Bright Stream said, "Do you think that we will shoot at each other always?"

"Not always," I said, but this is not what I believed. I believed that the killing would go on until there were no more Indians to kill. King James was determined to have all that her father owned, and arrows were no match for cannons.

Twenty-four

We left the Chesapeake and sailed up the James. The fort and barricades were stark against the April sky. As we tied up at the riverbank, Pocahontas hurried from the sterncastle, resplendent in a rabbit-fur cloak trimmed with weasel tails. At sight of her, Marshal Dale rushed to the ship's side. When Pocahontas reached the bank, he bowed and kissed her hand.

Before noon that day he moved out of his quarters in the fort and Pocahontas moved in. He assigned soldiers to guard her night and day and had a special cook prepare food from our meager supply that he hoped she would like.

A few settlers, those who had suffered under the Laws of Blood, noted how attentive he was. Emma Swinton said, "He's a snob, like all the other English gentlemen. He falls all over himself because she's royalty."

Marshal Dale was impressed by the fact that she was the daughter of a king. Her wild beauty enchanted him. And there was something else, far more important.

Before the day was out he sent a messenger up the James with a guard of well-armed soldiers. We knew what the message was before it ever left the town.

It bluntly said to Powhatan, supreme chieftain of the rivers, forests, and great lands of Tidewater Virginia, that his beloved daughter had been kidnapped. She was a prisoner of Marshal Dale in Jamestown and could be ransomed by the safe return of the seven Englishmen whom he held captive, the return of tools and muskets he had stolen, and a fulsome gift of corn as well. A prompt answer was suggested. In the meantime his daughter would be treated with the gentleness her position demanded.

A month went by but no formal answer came from the supreme chieftain.

However, a band of Indians attacked Henrico and burned down three of the new cabins, one of them near Tom Barlow's. Marshal Dale considered this an answer and raided a small village close to Henrico, shot two Indians, and captured four whom he set in the sun to dry out and die.

It was a tense time for the settlers, a trying time for me.

While Marshal Dale feuded with Powhatan, Captain Argall collected a load of timber from the pines that grew everywhere, tall and straight as arrows. It would be used in England for ship masts. He also took the first crop of tobacco John Rolfe and Tom Barlow had raised in Henrico. Having assumed I would return to England, he was surprised when I told him I had decided to wait until his next voyage.

"That will be six months from now, at least," he said. "You were so determined to leave. You're free to do so since you played a part in stealing the princess. What's happened?" He gave me a knowing glance. "Could it be Tom Barlow? I've seen you with him of late."

"Once, a month past."

"There's no harm in that. Barlow's not handsome, sort of plain, in fact. But this doesn't matter. He's a sturdy young man not afraid of work, which is unusual in Virginia."

"I don't have to leave now. You'll be making voyages

back and forth all year. I like Pocahontas. We're friends, and she needs a friend. If I leave, she'll have no one to talk to. Besides, our friendship could be helpful in Jamestown and Henrico, everywhere in Powhatan country."

"Indeed," Captain Argall said skeptically, unconvinced that this could be the reason for my wish to remain in Virginia.

I was silent, and let the captain think what he pleased about Tom Barlow.

"Barlow's coming down tomorrow with some of his fine timber. I trust you'll have time to see him."

"Oh, I'll see him. I always do when he comes here. I'm very fond of Tom. I've known him for a long, long time. We were shipwrecked together."

Tom did come down the river the following day, but he never made it to Jamestown. According to Stephen Turlock, who was traveling with him, he was towing a raft of timber, out in midstream, a more sensible place to be than along the shore, where he could easily be ambushed.

They had passed the mouth of a stream that runs into the James near Henrico. Two canoes they'd never seen slipped out behind them and unloosed a flight of arrows. One of the arrows struck Tom in the shoulder. They were much closer to Henrico than to Jamestown, so Turlock turned around, cut the timber loose, and paddled fast.

Harry Simpson, the barber, pulled out the arrow, and they carried Tom over to his cabin and made him comfortable. Simpson's wife stayed with him through the night.

When the news came early the next morning with the tide, Humility and I rowed up to Henrico. When we got there a fire was going, and Mistress Simpson had Tom lying bundled up in his big, wide bed. He was very pale. I thought he was dead. But he stirred when I called his name.

Barber Simpson's wife left us to go home and cook her husband's supper. She promised to return later that night if I thought I'd need her. I didn't. I went down to the river, brought back water to heat, and warmed up some venison soup Tom had left over.

He wouldn't eat any. He groaned all night but in the morning looked better and ate some of the soup. By noon he was talking—he always liked to talk—about the Indians who had ambushed him and about their leader.

"We know about Dale's message to Powhatan and Powhatan's answer," he said. "I suppose the arrow I received was part of it. Still, I believe we'll have peace. I've got faith in what Pocahontas can do. Do you suppose you could get her here somehow? It might be helpful. We'd get all the settlers together and sit down and talk."

"I'll try."

"But not until I'm back on my feet. Not before I get the place cleaned up a bit. I've been so busy with planting that I haven't had time to do anything around the cabin."

Humility and I had slept on the floor. Since it looked as if we would be needed for a few days, we went out in the woods and gathered leaves and boughs to sleep on.

Tom crawled out of his big bed, lay down on the pallet we had put together, and wouldn't move, though I raised my voice to him.

"I made the bed for you, you know," he said. "It's a good one. You may fall in love with it and decide to stay. Who knows? Women are funny sometimes. My sister Jenny married a man who raised tumbler pigeons because she liked to see them making somersaults in the sky. It gave her a religious feeling."

"I'm not going to fall in love with your bed, so get yourself in it and behave. You're still a sick man."

He obeyed me, so like a helpless child that a queer, protective feeling came over me, the first I had ever felt about him.

The barber came in the afternoon and dressed Tom's

wound, and his wife brought a parcel of food. Humility was fretting over what she was given to eat and wanted to go back to the fort.

Barber Simpson appeared every day to dress the wound, and his wife brought what food they could spare. After a week, Tom was sitting up, and I made plans to return to Jamestown. Then he came down with a fever.

Barber Simpson thought the arrow that struck Tom was poisoned. Tom went back to bed. I didn't leave, but I sent word to Pocahontas, who was still held at the fort, thinking she might know of an Indian remedy for his poisonous fever, if such it was.

At first, Marshal Dale, fearing that she might take a notion to flee, refused to let her leave. But she caused him all sorts of trouble, and he finally relented and sent her to Henrico, accompanied by a dozen guards.

When she came, she looked at Tom's eyes, his tongue, then his fingernails, and said that he had been poisoned. It was a poison that worked slowly and, if not treated, would eat away at him for years.

She searched the woods and came back with six kinds of milkweed, which she crushed and fed to him with water. This drug had to be given daily for at least a month. To find the various kinds of milkweed, to see that they were given promptly and in the right amount, she stayed on. Tom recovered a little every day.

Marshal Dale's guards killed a deer and gave us part of the meat. Barber Simpson's wife baked bread for us and brought news from Henrico and Jamestown. She told us that Powhatan had finally answered Marshal Dale.

Seven of our men had struggled into the fort, their muskets unusable, bearing a message: When Pocahontas was delivered, Powhatan would send five hundred bushels of corn and forever be a friend of the people in Jamestown and Henrico.

Marshal Dale answered at once, saying that the supreme chieftain had not returned everything, and until he did, his daughter would be held captive, gently withal.

One swooningly hot day while Tom was mending, Pocahontas and I were under an oak by the riverbank, away from the cruel sun. Her guards were not far off, dozing under another oak. Quietly, a canoe pulled ashore and John Rolfe got out, mopping his brow, praising the weather, saying it was fine for the tobacco crop.

He had not met Pocahontas. As I introduced them, he made a small nod and went on mopping his brow. But when she looked up at him, he put away his handkerchief, started to speak, then suddenly stopped, as if he had seen an apparition. His eyes closed and slowly opened.

He stayed only a short time, said little, and excused himself, saying the crops needed water. But he came to the cabin the next day, stayed longer, and talked some about tobacco.

The following day he appeared for supper, talked more about tobacco, then, seeing that Pocahontas was not interested, talked about England, but she was still quiet—I believe because England meant Captain John Smith, her dearest love.

As for John Rolfe, the wild beauty of the Indian girl, her glowing, boisterous spirit, so different from that of the frail, staid woman he had married, who lay buried in a James-town meadow, seized upon him. It blinded him to the point where he often fell speechless in her presence. He began to appear regularly at suppertime, would remain for supper, and leave late, finding his way in the night up the dark river.

When I learned to collect the six kinds of milkweed, make the paste, and give it in the right amount to our patient, Pocahontas went back to Jamestown with her guards, happy, I believe, to be away for a while from John Rolfe's attentions.

After a few more weeks of the milkweed treatment, Tom gained strength enough to go out to the fields. I got my things together and made a pack of the dolls he had fashioned from pine cones for Humility. He followed us to the river and helped us into the canoe. Humility brushed away tears. By now she liked Tom better than Marshal Dale.

"I'll fix up the cabin," Tom said. "Cobble a table and some chairs. They're making glass at Jamestown now. I'll get a piece and put in a proper window."

He gave the canoe a shove and it picked up the current.

"I'll get some cloth and make a curtain, too," he called. "So the Indians can't look in."

"I'll make the curtain," I called back. "I'll send it along."

"Bring it," he shouted.

Twenty-five

T wice each week, Rolfe came down from Henrico, forty miles by the river, double the distance by forest trail, to see Pocahontas. On these lonely trips back and forth he must have suffered, if one could judge by his haggard looks, the awful pains of damnation.

The first word I heard of his torment was on a day of lowering clouds. He had already come down the river two times that week. This was the third time. I was outside washing clothes, spreading them on the bushes to dry, when he called me aside.

"Have you seen her today?" he asked.

"Yes, we ate together this morning," I said.

"Did she bring up my name?"

"Yes, once."

"In what way?"

"She said you had proposed marriage."

"What will she answer, do you think? I couldn't tell what she thought."

"She looks upon you favorably."

Relief shone in his tormented eyes, but almost at once a shadow settled upon them. He was a Calvinist, familiar with the warnings of the Old Testament. In Henrico he led us in prayer at supper and often quoted passages from the Bible.

But I was astounded to hear him say, staring into the stormy heavens, "I am terribly aware of the displeasure which Almighty God conveyed against the sons of Israel for marrying strange wives."

Did he think upon Pocahontas as strange? Was it possible?

"I have moments when I fear my relations with her are more demonic than divine," he said. "Is it God or Satan who has provoked me to be in love with one whose education has been so rude or absent, her manners barbarous, her generation cursed and so different in all ways from my own? Surely these are instigations hatched by him who seeks and delights in men's destruction."

I was astounded at this outburst. I hoped that Pocahontas would send him packing. What effrontery! What arrogance! For the first time I saw clearly the gulf that separated us from the Indians. How could there ever be peace between us while white men looked upon the red men as barbarians, a group to exploit and to murder, if necessary?

Rolfe's private torment became a public scandal. Divided among themselves about God and His Word, the settlers agreed upon one thing. The marriage of John Rolfe to an Indian would be a mortal sin.

Emma Swinton was certain that Rolfe consorted with the devil. In fact, she had seen the two of them riding in the same canoe.

"He sits in the stern, wrapped in a fur-trimmed cloak with a large black hood, whether the day is cold or hot," she said. "In his hand there's always a Bible, from which he reads in mocking tones, twisting the words to suit his evil schemes." Her gray face turned reddish. "I have seen

Satan, I swear, and heard his monstrous voice. Burn me if I lie."

The proposed marriage seemed sinful to Marshal Dale, who in his zeal had set down a list of blue laws to match his blood laws. Church attendance twice each day he had made compulsory. If a man or woman failed in this, he or she gave up a week's food allowance. A second offense brought a serious flogging. Those who persisted were hanged, shot, or burned at the stake. Profanity was punished by a lash or a hot bodkin run through the tongue.

Marshal Dale, noted as a leader in Christian matters, abhorred the scandal. He put his sharp mind to the problem and came up with an idea. Since Pocahontas lacked a soul, he would find her one. To this end, he appointed Master Whitaker, a young man of twenty-six steeped in the Bible.

Pocahontas was whisked away to Henrico.

The skimpy fringed dress that failed to cover half her beauty was discarded. She was stuffed into a bone corset, covered from waist to ankle in a farthingale, a stiff framework draped with crinoline, and sent away to the Reverend Whitaker's hundred-acre parsonage to become a Christian.

I didn't see her while I was making the curtain for Tom's cabin. No word came to Jamestown about her except that she was an apt pupil and was fast learning Christian ways.

I had forgotten to measure the cabin window, so Humility and I visited the glassmaker to find out the size Tom had bought. It was two feet high and two feet wide. Then we went to the ship's storeroom for fabric. I couldn't find the material I wanted—brown bombazine with yellow flowers spread around in a cheerful pattern. There was nothing remotely like this. Indeed, all they could offer was a length of plain white netting.

"You might try Henrico," the clerk said. "There's a new

shop on River Lane. It sells everything in the way of cloth. Tell them James Armbruster sent you."

As we were leaving, Emma Swinton spoke up. It was not a chance meeting. I had seen her come up the gangplank and follow me in. She had been hiding somewhere in the storeroom.

"I have just the thing for a curtain," she said, speaking in her soft voice, which was like the hissing of a gentle snake. "I brought it all the way from London." From under her cloak she removed a parcel of cloth and spread it out on the counter. The light in the storeroom was poor but the cloth glittered like the purest gold.

"The cabin's dark," I said. "Your cloth is just the thing to liven it up. How much do you ask?"

"Nothing, 'tis a wedding gift. But now and then you must let me keep the girl," she said, pinching Humility's ear. "There are things I wish to teach her."

"Wedding gift? I am not marrying Tom Barlow. Whenever did you unearth that idea?"

"Before the hurricane, long ago, the night you wandered out on deck, and Tom Barlow talked to you about St. Elmo's fire."

"I didn't know Tom then. I had never spoken to him before. I madly loved Anthony Foxcroft."

Her eyes turned inward. Their mottled whites were all that I could see. "The future casts a backward glance," she said. "The past casts a forward glance. Fiery Aldebaran leads the unshorn sheep to pasture."

I made nothing of her words, no more than I usually did. But on closer look I saw that woven into the silk were tiny stars. It was the stars that lent the cloth a golden glister.

"You're most welcome to it. And I'll be most happy to help. I am a seamstress by trade. For years I served Lady Pamela—"

Her breath caught in her throat.

The name Pamela stirred memories. I recalled that a year before I left Foxcroft, a Lady Pamela Moss had fallen from a window in Moss Castle. Her seamstress was accused of pushing Lady Pamela to her death. It was a celebrated trial. King James himself had directed it, standing by the rack and asking questions. Certain that she was a witch, the king had the seamstress stretched on the rack. But the trial, for all the stretching, ended in acquittal.

Had Emma Swinton been Lady Pamela's seamstress? It could account for her knobby wrists, the hissing sound she made when talking, her bulging eyes streaked like agates.

"Do you wish me to help?" she asked in a plaintive voice.

"No," I said, suddenly blindingly aware that the making of the curtain was an act of love. "Thank you, but I wish to sew it myself. And thank you for the cloth. It will be beautiful at the window. I hope he will like it. He has simple tastes and this isn't simple. It's elegant."

"It should be. It came from a cardinal's robe taken from the vestry."

I made the curtain much longer and wider than the window. I cut and sewed it myself, though Emma offered suggestions. I couldn't refuse her when she asked to accompany Humility and me to Henrico.

On the way we stopped at the parsonage. The Reverend Whitaker appeared at the courtyard gate. He was sorry that Rebecca could not be seen.

"Rebecca?" I said. "What an outlandish name for an Indian girl."

"She's deep in her studies," he said. "A visit with you, I fear, would prove an unwanted distraction."

"But, Master Whitaker, we're friends, old friends."

"Yes, that's precisely why your presence here will remind her of those pagan days."

Yet as he shuffled his feet, he seemed to waver. Then his

gaze fell upon the forbidding figure of Emma Swinton. He frowned and in one motion bowed himself through the gate, saying, "I'll inform Rebecca that you came."

We had not gone far along the path that led to the river when I heard footsteps. Through the trees, her hair streaming, Pocahontas burst upon us.

"You're going to Tom Barlow's. I'll go with you," she said, and running ahead, urged us on. "Hurry. Reverend Whitaker will come looking."

I stopped where I was. She had a small bundle in her arms. "You're not fleeing?" I said, alarmed. "If you are, they'll surely find you and blame us."

"No. Reverend Whitaker is a kind man, but the name Rebecca I do not like and I am tired of the books I do not understand and all the candles that smoke, and kind Reverend Whitaker gliding around full of smiles. I would like to smell the sea wind again and take off these clothes and swim in the river and shout Indian words to the great Manitou."

"Once a wild Indian, always a wild Indian," Emma Swinton said, but took her by the hand, and the two began to run, Humility crying for them to wait.

Twenty-six

We hurried out of sight. Time would pass, perhaps hours, before the Reverend Whitaker would discover that Pocahontas had gone. Even then, it would take him a while to find her.

When we got to the far side of the river, she slipped out of her taffeta dress, kicked off her ribboned shoes and stood naked. With a whoop she slid into the river, disappeared, and came up spouting water. She glowed in the sun. She looked like a forest animal and sounded like one.

Humility wanted to follow her. I put an end to this and kept watch on the opposite shore. No one was in sight, but up the river I made out a dim shape, what I took to be a fleet of Indian canoes. I couldn't tell whether they were moving in our direction.

By the time Pocahontas came out of the water, opened the bundle she had brought, and put on a leather shirt, the canoes were closer but still at some distance.

"Mattaponi," she said.

"How do you know?" I asked her.

"They're painted black and have white faces and their canoes are black."

"Who are they?"

"They live on a stream to the north. The Mattaponi were my father's good friends. They got mad at him and have become our enemies. They are on a raid and not to be trusted. We will hide our canoe. We'll cover our tracks with dirt until we're in the forest."

It was midafternoon and very hot. Tom was in the field hoeing plants. He dropped the hoe and trotted down the path to meet us. The long summer had bronzed his skin. He looked like an Indian.

"Did you bring food?" were his first words. "The cupboard's bare. It's been bare for two days now. I planned a trip to town this afternoon."

"The woods are overrunning with deer and turkey," Emma said. "Why do you not shoot yourself something to eat?"

"Because I'm low on powder and lead. I'd rather go hungry than run out of shot."

"Find me some willows," Pocahontas said, "and I'll show you how to make a rabbit trap."

Pocahontas was in a happy mood. I think it was because she had escaped from the Reverend Whitaker's parsonage. I had never seen her so happy, so happy or so beautiful. Her dark eyes glowed. Her long black hair, still wet from the river, shone in the sun.

Once inside, she ran to the big copper pan that Tom had hung on the wall and parted her hair in three heavy braids. She twisted them together and piled them around her head in a rough coronet. Then she surveyed herself, turning her head from side to side. She was beautiful. What's more, she knew she was beautiful and reveled in it.

Humility went out and came back with willow branches, which Pocahontas trimmed and tied together with a thong from her skirt.

Tom thanked her, but he wasn't much interested in the

trap. He kept glancing at me when he thought I wasn't looking. And he kept this up while Emma opened her bundle and passed around corncakes and speckled turkey eggs and muscadine grapes. He still didn't know about the curtain.

I waited until the last crumb was eaten and Humility had made a drink of muscadine juice and cold spring water, a drink she made at Jamestown and loved. Only then did I take out the curtain. Tom had put two pegs on either side of the window and a peeled branch between.

"A perfect fit," Tom said.

He did a little dance. He lit two candles because the curtain had darkened the room. Then we danced and sang. Humility had the only good voice among us, clear and true and touching.

Emma was the only one who didn't sing. She went to the window, opened the curtain, and looked out. At what, I do not know—perhaps the green fields, the skies that were turning gray, the brooding forest where the last of the sun clung to the topmost branches.

It was almost dark when the face appeared at the window. At first I thought that the Reverend Whitaker had come for Pocahontas. She saw the face, quickly drew the curtain, then ran to the door. It was closed but not locked. She lifted the wooden bar, slid it into place, and blew out the two candles.

"Mattaponi," Pocahontas whispered to Tom.

Above the room was a loft. I lifted Humility and put her into it and told her to be quiet. Tom parted the curtain a crack. Through the trees a heavy moon was rising. A wind had come up. A light knock sounded at the door, then three knocks, each louder than the one before.

"Who are you?" Tom asked.

"Seanoc speaks for werowance of the Mattaponi."

"What do you want?"

"Werowance comes for the daughter of evil Powhatan."

"She is not here," Tom replied. "Go to the parsonage across the river and see Reverend Whitaker."

I heard feet running. The sounds seemed to come from all sides of the cabin. Dozens of Indians must have been there in the moonlight. The man who spoke for the werowance was silent.

"Do you understand my talk?" Tom said.

"Understand good," the man said.

"Then what are you waiting for?"

"For Pocahontas," the man said. "We follow Pocahontas from place across river, up here. Understand?"

Tom took down his musket from the mantelpiece. He poured powder from his powder horn into the barrel, set a wad of cloth on top, packed the powder down hard, and sprinkled some in the powder pan.

"I understand," he said.

There was a long silence. Then a different Indian, one with a raspy voice, spoke haughtily, his words so loud and fast that Tom didn't understand them. Pocahontas whispered that it was the werowance speaking, that he had heard about the kidnapping and the ransom the white man, Dale, had demanded.

"He thinks that what the white man can do, the Mattaponi can do," she said.

"What you can do is to be wise," Tom called to the werowance. "Leave here before Pocahontas comes. She comes soon with many guards. They will hack you down with sharp swords and throw your bodies in the river for the big fish and the small fish to eat."

"Ho," the werowance called back, "we see what big fish and small fish eat."

There was another silence, broken by nighthawk cries, cries the nighthawks did not make. I parted the curtain and peered out.

"The werowance has left the door," I said. "At the edge of the clearing, where the forest begins, black figures are dancing around a fire."

Tom came to the window. "The werowance," he said, "is among them in his feathered robe and eagle feathers, trying hard to decide if it's wise to set fire to the cabin. If he does, Pocahontas might be killed. He doesn't care about us."

Humility had stopped crying, but when she heard Tom's frightening words she let out a sob. I quieted her by lifting her down from the loft. She got in the bed, disappeared in the covers, and lay quiet.

The werowance returned. "Daughter of King Powhatan," he said in his raspy voice, "do you come out like a princess, head high, or am I to set fire to the cabin and burn you out like a little rat?"

She was stung by his words. Color showed in her cheeks. "You know my father," she said. "You know he is a vengeful man. You need no proof of that. He slew three of your brothers by removing their skins from head to toe with the sharpened edge of clam shells. If you harm me, if you harm my friends, he will hunt you down wherever you may hide and do the same to you."

"Your father grows old, feeble, a little crazy," the werowance said. "I fear him not."

Again I looked through the part in the curtain. Behind the werowance stood a row of warriors carrying fagots that gave off fire and smoke.

The wind drove wisps of the smoke under the door. Emma, who was sitting on the bed, trying to calm Humility, began to cough. She got up and came over to us.

"What do you propose to do?" she said to Pocahontas, speaking peremptorily, as if there were many choices. "We can't just stand around and breathe pine smoke and wait to be burned up, can we?"

Pocahontas ignored her and said to the werowance, "You followed me from the place across the river. I was taken there by white warriors with iron muskets that shoot fire, not with wood clubs. Those white warriors are looking for me now. They'll see your canoes on the shore. They'll come here. And that will be the end of you."

"I just heard this," the werowance said. "The man told me guards are here soon. The moon is overhead. Guards have not come. Maybe they are afraid to come."

No one spoke. In the silence I heard footsteps scurrying across the roof. Then there was a loud noise in the chimney. Suddenly a fagot struck the hearthstone and sparks flew into the room.

Emma Swinton stamped them out. Tom held a matchlock in the crook of his arm; his other gun hung above the mantel. Emma took it down.

"Is it ready to shoot?" she asked him.

"Except for the priming."

"It's time to prime it," she said.

Tom tested the flint, sprinkled powder in the priming pan, and leaned the musket against the door. Emma picked it up and swung it around, aiming at the door, at the window, finally at him. He took it away from her and set it against the wall.

Another fagot fell down the chimney. The first one was still smoldering, giving off puffs of black smoke. The second one showered sparks and began to smolder. A third fagot came clattering to the hearth.

None of the smoke went up the chimney. After they tossed a fagot, they covered the chimney top. The werowance had no intention of setting the cabin on fire, running the risk of losing Pocahontas. Instead, he was bent upon smoking her out.

The Indians danced around outside. There were more sounds on the roof and three more fagots came down the chimney.

Clearing his throat, the werowance said, "Good news. Guards of big place beyond the river have torches. They will march to the river. They will get in their canoes. As the sun rises they will come. Too late. I will be gone away. Gone with daughter of Powhatan, Powhatan who is so ugly I wonder he had such a beautiful girl. Crazy, is this ugly Powhatan."

The werowance made a sniffing noise. "I smell some smoke," he said. "A good smell. Like pine forest on a summer day. You smell it, too, in there?"

No one answered. The smoke was so heavy in the room we barely could see each other. Humility, who had been lying rigid under a blanket, put her head out, but as another fagot fell and her eyes began to smart, she covered herself again.

I sat down on the bed beside her. Surely the guards were on their way from the parsonage. They would not wander around all night looking for Pocahontas, as the werowance said. The Reverend Whitaker would tell them that she was probably with me at Tom Barlow's.

The air became hard to breathe. Everyone was coughing. A bucket of water sat under the table. Emma groped her way through the smoke, picked it up, and threw water on the fagot, but it only sizzled and made more smoke.

"You look very calm," she said to me. "In no time at all I'll be dead while you calmly sit."

She stared at the serpent ring. "You are calm because of that," she said, biting her words. "Calm because it will save you." She reached down and grasped my hand. She tried to wrench the ring from my finger. Failing, she dealt me a slap on the cheek.

"Coward!" she shouted.

The insult rang loud in my ears, like a clap of thunder. I said nothing. It stunned me. I rose to my feet and faced her. Still I was silent. Suddenly I thought: She is right. I do feel calm. I do feel safe. While my accuser, while Tom Barlow and Pocahontas and Humility cowering under her blanket, face death.

I got to my feet and found the fireplace. I threw the ring into the fire. I went to my copper pan hanging on the wall; smoke had dimmed its luster.

I wiped the smoke off with my sleeve and looked at myself. The king's mark, the bloody smudge that had never left me since the morning it was placed there, that I had tried to wash away time after time, the sign no one on the ship or in Bermuda or Jamestown had ever been able to see, was gone.

Another fagot, the largest of all, came down the chimney and rolled into the room. The child was safe for a moment under her heavy blanket. But the others were at the door.

Pocahontas said, "The werowance is right about the guards. They will be here but, traveling in the dark, not before morning."

"We'll not last that long," Tom said. "I'll go outside and talk to the werowance. While I talk, try to slip away and hide in the woods."

He reached for the latch, but Pocahontas grasped his arm and, holding him back, opened the door and went out. A gust of wind blew through the cabin. The fagot that lay on the floor burst into flames. I gathered Humility in my arms. Beyond the doorway Pocahontas was talking to the werowance. I called to her but she did not answer.

Emma passed me, dragging the matchlock. At the door she struggled to raise the heavy gun, took careless aim, and pressed the trigger. Not a sound, not a word, came from the werowance as he toppled backward and lay very still.

Arrows and howls filled the night. One of the arrows was afire. I saw it coming through the sky. It was coming straight toward me, slowly, in a flaming arc. I had time to stand out of its way, but I could not move. For a fleeting moment I thought of the serpent ring and regretted that I had thrown it away. With a fiery sound, shedding sparks, the arrow grazed my cheek and passed harmlessly away.

Now that the werowance was dead, his warriors ran for the river, yelling as they went. We huddled in the moonlight, watching the cabin burn to the ground, taking half the tobacco plants with it.

At dawn the guards marched up from the river. Pocahontas heard them before they reached the clearing.

"Tell them I am eating my breakfast with Reverend Whitaker," she said, laughing as she ran.

"Good riddance," Emma Swinton said.

Ashes smoldered in the rising sun. The chimney stood tall and straight against the sky. But the pine logs hewn so carefully, the little window, the curtain, the big wide bed, were gone.

Tom said, "I have work to do."

"*We* have work to do," I corrected him.

He smiled and picked me up, with Humility in my arms, and whirled us around.

"When do we begin?" I asked.

"We could start today," Tom said. "Except the ashes are too blasted hot."

Twenty-seven

Pocahontas was back with the Reverend Whitaker by noon. Tom and I, worried that by some ill chance she might have been captured by the Mattaponi, went across the river to the parsonage. We found her eating a hearty meal of quail and cornbread, while the Reverend looked on with tight lips.

Later he prevailed upon us to stay for a service, it being Sunday. A goodly number of Henrico's settlers were there, including John Rolfe, who sat hand in hand with Pocahontas. The Reverend read from a Bible Captain Argall had brought from England.

I was so excited by what I heard that afterward I told the Reverend Whitaker that it sounded like the Bible I had grown up with—the New Testament William Tyndale had translated.

"Yes, that was a hundred years ago," the Reverend said. "This is a new Bible. It's just been published. King James chose some scholars and they put their heads together and brought forth this one. It's called the King James Bible."

"King James really did this?"

"It was his idea and he did it."

I wondered how the man who believed in witches and took delight in punishing them with leg irons and racks could be responsible for such splendor.

"But it sounds like Tyndale," I said. "It sings like his Bible."

"It should," Reverend Whitaker said. "More than half is Tyndale. I have counted. I spent time counting the Sermon on the Mount. Two hundred eighty-seven words in the Sermon are from William Tyndale.

"And he was burned at the stake for his labor."

Months later, when Tom and I were married, the Reverend Whitaker read from the new King James Bible. His pleasant voice soared through the chapel. The words possessed wings. They made up for the lack of flowers, the storm that piled snow against the parsonage walls and closed most of the roads so that few of our neighbors could come.

Two months later, when John Rolfe and Pocahontas were married, things were far different. The wedding took place in the Jamestown church. It was April and the church was filled with wildflowers. Bells announced the wedding. Everyone came, even the bride's uncle, Opitchapan, and two of her young brothers. The Reverend Bucke beamed from the pulpit.

Her clothes, unlike mine, were elaborate and new. She wore a white muslin tunic, a trailing veil, and a long pink robe. Around her neck was a double chain of pearls, a handsome gift from her father who, though he approved of the marriage, had proudly refused to attend.

Never had I seen a happier man than John Rolfe, unless it was my Tom Barlow. Pocahontas seemed happy, too. They went to live in a house on the James River, near Henrico, on land Chief Powhatan had given them. Rolfe called their new house Varina after a variety of tobacco brought from Spain.

With the wedding, a sort of peace settled upon the colony.

Everyone was pleased, except King James. When he was informed of the marriage, he fell into a violent fit and accused Rolfe of high treason for marrying the daughter of a savage king.

With his hand on his heart, he angrily promised that no offspring of John Rolfe would ever inherit a foot of Virginia land. But when he was told that the eight chieftains of the Powhatan Confederacy were ready to sign peace treaties, he had second thoughts. When told that his picture would be scribed on copperplate and presented to the chieftains to wear round their necks on heavy copper chains, he was flattered. Grudgingly, he consented to Rolfe's marriage to Pocahontas, though she was still a barbarian and lacked a soul.

Varina was not far from our home, a short canoe ride and a mile's walk, so I saw Pocahontas every week or two. When she first moved to Varina she visited us and, unbeknownst to her husband, brought four of his special Spanish tobacco roots, which she showed Tom how to plant.

I was surprised when the Rolfes sailed off to England with their new son and a retinue of ten tribespeople, men and women. I was fearful that something might happen to her in that land of somber skies.

Word came from time to time about her, but long after things had happened, there being few ships from England at this time. A letter written by Captain John Smith introduced her to Queen Anne. She was a guest at court functions and lordly festivities. Her portrait was painted by a famous artist. Engravings were made of it and one was sent to Jamestown.

She was wearing a mantle of red velvet and a dark underdress festooned with gold buttons and a lacy collar. Banded with gold, her hat had the look of a jaunty coronet. Her black hair was masked by a reddish wig that I assumed must be popular among London's high-born ladies.

Gazing at the portrait, which had been hung above Sir Thomas Dale's fireplace, I was impressed by her beauty. But in her eyes I detected a hint of sadness.

Word came that she had grown tired of the gala affairs. Her health was suffering from London's damp air. She had moved to the country, where streams of courtiers unfortunately still visited her. It was here, we learned, that she met Captain John Smith again and was so overcome with emotion she could not speak.

Good news came. Her health had improved, and Ben Jonson's Christmas masque was performed on Twelfth-night in her honor. Two months passed before a ship brought word that she was ill again and had taken to her bed. Then we heard that she and her family had gone to Gravesend, at the mouth of the Thames, ready to leave on the first ship that sailed for Virginia. What happy news!

Tom and I were in the field planting a crop of timothy hay when the last word came. The April sun was bright. There was a sweet smell in the air of forest and sea, the sweet smell of Virginia in the spring.

The Reverend Whitaker brought the news. He came slowly up the path from the river. He looked at us a moment and swallowed.

"She has gone," he said. "We will not see her ever in this life again. But she is safe with God and one day we will see her." He stopped and could speak no more.

"Come and sit," Tom said.

"She is Virginia," the Reverend Whitaker said.

"Yes," Tom said. "There would be none without her."

We walked through the new-sown field toward the cabin. As we walked, I saw her at the cabin door. She was clear as the April day, standing with her long legs thrust apart, her hands on her hips, watching us with her Indian eyes.

Author's Note

Serena Lynn is an imaginary character, suggested in appearance and deportment by Mary Riverdale, a lithesome member of the king's court. Through Serena's eyes we see the founding of America.

Sir Walter Raleigh's two attempts to found a colony at Roanoke Island in Virginia, in 1585 and 1587, failed. Both colonies disappeared without a trace. But in 1606 King James granted a charter to the Virginia Company of London to found a colony, and the following year more than a hundred settlers disembarked at Jamestown. This was thirteen years before the Pilgrims landed at Plymouth Rock.

In writing the story of Jamestown and Pocahontas, I have depended upon a number of books, booklets, tracts, journals, and letters. Among the booklets are *A Voyage to Virginia in 1609*, edited by Louis B. Wright, and Terry Tucker's *Bermuda—Unintended Destination*. Books I used were Otto J. Scott's notable biography of James I, the adventurous *Three Worlds of Captain John Smith*, by Philip L. Barbour, and Francis Mossiker's *Pocahontas*, a fine picture of early Virginia and the life of its legendary princess. Captain John Smith's original *Generall Historie of Virginia, New-England, and the Summer Isles*, printed in 1624 when the letter *s* looked like the letter *f*, is hard to read but most rewarding. A streamlined edition, in which the letter *s* looks like the letter *s*, is now available.

Among the letters are ones written by Sir Thomas Gates, governor of Virginia; by Edmon Scott, a member of the Virginia Company of London; by Gabriel Archar, on board the *Blessing*, a ship in the Virginia Fleet of 1609; and by William Strachey, secretary-elect to Virginia.

Strachey's letter has an interesting history. It was written from Jamestown to a mysterious woman in London, whom he addresses as "Excellent Lady" and "Noble Lady." The letter contains a dramatic description of the storm that overtook the *Sea Venture*, one of the ships in the Virginia fleet. A description so dramatic that the Noble Lady passed the letter on to her friend, William Shakespeare.

Shakespeare, it is rumored, was so taken by Strachey's description of the storm that he had Miranda echo it in a scene from *The Tempest*:

> ". . . wild waters in this roar, allay them.
> The sky, it seems, would pour down stinking pitch,
> . . . .
> Had I been any god of power, I would
> Have sunk the sea within the earth or ere
> It should the good ship so have swallow'd and
> The fraughting souls within her."

John Rolfe's apology for marrying Pocahontas is taken word for word from one of his letters. The thoughts of King James on smoking are also reported word for word. Other details, difficult to put in the story, cropped up.

The settlers thought they were dying from some awful plague. We know now that they died from salt poisoning.

Salt from the sea swept in with the tides and poisoned the river water they drank.

Admiral Sir George Somers, dear friend of Serena, sailed back to Bermuda, narrowly escaping death in a storm, only soon to die there. His body was sent to England, but his heart was buried on the island.

Henry Ravens and his crew were never heard of again.

About the Author

SCOTT O'DELL is a Newbery Medalist, a three-time Newbery Honor Book winner, and the recipient of various other awards including the Hans Christian Andersen Author Medal, the highest international recognition for a body of work by an author of children's books.

Other Scott O'Dell books for Fawcett Juniper are ALEXANDRA; THE CASTLE IN THE SEA; THE ROAD TO DAMIETTA; THE SPANISH SMILE; STREAMS TO THE RIVER, RIVERS TO THE SEA; and THE SERPENT NEVER SLEEPS.

Mr. O'Dell died in 1989.